IRREPRESSIBLE

BOOK 5

THE BLOODLUST CHRONICLES

TARA VASSER

Copyright© Winter Musings LLC **2017** Copyright info: Winter Musings LLC
15310 Taylor St NE
Ham Lake, MN 55304

978-1-947882-03-4 PRINT

978-1-947882-04-1 EBOOK - MOBI

978-1-947882-05-8 EBOOK - EPUB

978-1-947882-06-5 AUDIOBOOK

Editing By: There for You Editing

Cover Art By: DuskTilDawn Designs

Photo Credit:

Royal Touch Photography

IRREPRESSIBLE

IRREPRESSIBLE IS A NOVELLA SET IN PARALLEL TO EVENTS IN IRRECOVERABLE (BOOK 4). IT IS WRITTEN TO BE READ FOLLOWING ENJOYMENT OF IRRESISTIBLE (BOOK 1), IRREDEEMABLE (BOOK 2), IRREPLACEABLE (BOOK 3), AND IRRECOVERABLE (BOOK 4).

DEDICATION

To Tony – My love for you is Irrepressible.

Acknowledgements

Special thanks go out to:

Ashley, what would I do without you, really?

Jen for providing constructive criticism, I appreciate your candor!

Johanna for the beautiful photos.

Henry for bringing Zeke to life!

Royal Touch Photography. The photo turned out so much better than my idea.

Dusk Til Dawn Designs for allowing me to put your art onto my books.

Melissa for being the voice of reason when I've read the book so many times I can't see straight.

My awesome readers. Just the fact you are reading this allows me to keep going. Never underestimate how important you are to me!

IRREPRESSIBLE

Having men invade her house should have been terrifying enough for Jody Matthews, but finding out they were not human took it to a whole new level. Helpless and at the mercy of ruthless Vampires, she learns she is a bargaining chip in a struggle she can't even begin to understand.

Just when Jody begins to believe she will either fall victim to the obsessed Vampire who has been stalking her in past weeks and is now professing love, or the sadistic Vampire hell-bent on drawing pained screams from her, a third Vampire enters the equation.

Whisked away from the nightmare occupying her house, Jody is rescued by Zeke, a Vampire with a penchant for aiding damsels in distress. After losing their only means of communication with Jody's sister—Zeke's phone—the Vampire brings her to his home while they formulate a plan. In such close quarters, will Jody be able to resist his charm and repress the feelings he evokes in her?

CHAPTER ONE

Jody groaned as her phone pinged. *Again.* When the last message came through, she'd vowed to ignore it, but, like some kind of compulsion, she picked up the device and swiped across the screen to see what it said anyway. It was the same conversation her and her best friend seemed to have nearly every night.

Bri: But there's this really cute guy.

Jody shook her head in exasperation. She would have thought by now that her track record of declining the vast majority of Bri's invitations to bar hop in Minneapolis would be a pretty good indicator that tonight's partying was a no go. She had a shift at the hospital tomorrow, and all she wanted to do tonight was relax and ignore the frigid weather awaiting her outside her front door.

Jody: I'm already in my PJs.

Bri: Jo! Ur not a bear! Ppl don't hibernate just bcuz it's winter!

Jody: I'm just going to stay in tonight. Waiting for Alicia.

Bri: How are you ever going to get laid if you don't come out?

Shaking her head at the last comment, Jody threw her phone to the side. Bri should know by now that trying to argue Jody out of the house when it was cold and dark outside was an exercise in futility. She was a homebody at the best of times, and basically a hermit when the temperature dropped below freezing. Most times she questioned her sanity for living someplace where the air hurt her face half the year, but then the rest of the time she remembered it was so she could remain close to her sister.

Jody's phone pinged once more, and she praised herself for the solid minute she ignored it and focused her attention on her movie. It pinged again, and she picked it up for the same reason she always did—in the off chance it might be her sister, Alicia. Not a day went by she didn't at least message with her sister, let alone talk. Sometimes the messages consisted solely of emojis, but it was always something. Except today. It was already almost eleven at night, and Alicia still hadn't responded to Jody's DVD + wolf face emoji message which was their standard encryption for suggesting a *Game of Thrones* marathon. Winter had come and they needed to show their loyalty to their King in the North by watching and re-watching Jon Snow and all his glory on her tiny TV.

A loud knock at the door startled Jody, making her jump and bite into her bottom lip where she'd been worrying it between her teeth.

"Dammit!" she cursed, wiping her thumb across the bead of blood and looking at it. Damned dry winter air could split her lips within a few hours if she didn't apply lip balm religiously. "Be right there!" she called when another insistent knock sounded.

Perplexed, she made her way cautiously to the door, trying to make out the shape of whoever it was through the frosted sidelight. She wasn't expecting anyone ... well, except maybe her sister, but Alicia never knocked. She walked right in, and if the door was still locked, she used the spare key Jody had given her for just such an emergency as when she was too lazy to dig herself out from under a mound of blankets. Jody placed her hand on the door handle just as her cat, Plato, darted in front of her feet, intent on making his escape into the frozen night.

"Not a chance," Jody mumbled to him as she scooped him up into her arms.

Pulling the door open a crack, she peered out at the man standing on her front stoop. She didn't recognize him at all, so she was relieved for the small barrier her screen provided should this guy be some kind of crazy. She didn't exactly live in the boonies, but her nearest neighbors did live about a quarter of a mile down the road. Alicia had been miffed when she'd bought the small house outside the cities and the ring of suburbs, but Jody enjoyed the seclusion and the yard for her gardening hobby when everything wasn't covered in snow. It was times like these, though, when strange men appeared at her door at night that she had a niggling feeling Alicia was at least a little bit right about it being dangerous for a woman to live alone out here.

"Can I help you?" Jody asked cautiously.

"I certainly hope so," the man responded with a cordial grin that sent shivers down her spine.

Plato hissed and spit in her arms, and her attention was drawn away from the man at her door for a moment while she attempted to situate the cat in her arms to where his sharp claws didn't tear into her.

"Are you the sister of Alicia Matthews?"

Jody's heart stopped at the mention of her sister's name. A million scenarios flew through her head that all involved her sister injured, dying, or dead and that's why she never answered Jody's message today.

"Is she okay?" Jody inquired frantically, losing her grip on the cat.

Plato growled and launched himself from her arms, his back claws creating deep gouges in her forearm she hardly noticed while she waited for the man to answer her question.

The man smiled at her, and it was more cold than friendly. From out of the darkness, two men appeared next to him, sending more shivers down her spine.

"I'm sorry, who are you?" she asked, reaching to make sure the screen door was locked. It wouldn't do much to keep any of these guys out, but it should at least give her a few seconds to close the heavy steel door and lock it before they could get through.

"Acquaintances of your sister's." The man reached for the handle to the screen door.

"I think you should come back tomorrow," Jody told him, unable to keep her voice from shaking.

"I think we'll come in and stay a while," he countered, his cordial smile morphing into one of pure menace.

Jody's eyes went wide and she rushed to close the door and lock it like she'd planned, but before she could so much as take a step back, one of the men from the flanks had pulled open the screen door with almost no effort despite the lock there, and the other pushed the door she still held. The force of his push propelled her backward and toward the floor with a screech. However, before she could hit the tile and sustain bruises, one of the men grabbed her and pulled her to her feet roughly.

"Hey!" A powerful arm snaked around her waist and pinned her arms to her sides. "Who are you? What do you want?" she screamed at them, her voice bordering on hysteria.

The two remaining men filed into her entryway, closing the door behind them. Out on her front stoop, they'd looked frightening, but with their towering frames hulking over her in the small space of her foyer, they were positively terrifying.

The man who spoke on the stoop turned in a slow circle, surveying the small entry and the rooms beyond. His face was void of all emotion, but his eyes, when they stopped on Jody, were filled with a mixture of annoyance and distaste. His gaze raked over her from head to toe in an assessment filled with coldness rivaling the howling wind outside.

"Tie her up and put her somewhere else. I don't want to see or hear her," he ordered dispassionately and turned away.

"What do you want?" Jody yelled, trying to struggle from the grip of the man who held her tight against his chest. But she might as well have been trying to bend the iron bars of a jail cell for all the good it did her.

The ringleader turned around quickly, anger flashing in his dark eyes. Jody attempted to shrink away from the malevolence there, but there was nowhere to go with the real-life personification of The Mountain behind her holding her firm. The ringleader gripped her jaw painfully, and as much as she tried to hold in her cry, it slipped out.

"I want something from your sister. You are our insurance policy that she does what I have requested," he sneered, giving her jaw a squeeze that drew a whimper from her. "Get her out of my sight," he ordered the mountain holding her.

Mountain Man picked her up like she weighed nothing, and Jody screamed when her feet left the ground.

"Put me do—" she started, but her scream was cut off when his big hand slapped across her mouth, making her wince at the sting of the contact.

The man carried her up the stairs toward the bedrooms amidst her muffled screams behind his hand.

"Rodriguez," the ringleader called from behind them, and the man carrying her stopped short, but didn't turn. "No fucking and no biting."

Rodriguez didn't acknowledge the order before he wordlessly continued his ascent toward the bedrooms. Jody continued to scream and kicked out her legs, trying to connect with his balls, his shins, *anything,* but the damned man was strong enough he just tilted her away from his body, and instead she ended up kicking the banister and stubbing her toe. Somehow, it still managed to hurt worse than the pain radiating from her jaw.

CHAPTER TWO

The man called Rodriguez dropped Jody on the bed, and she scrambled as quickly as she could to get across to the other side, but didn't make it more than a few inches before he got ahold of her ankle. *Damn he's fast. And strong.* Clawing at the comforter, Jody attempted to slow her acceleration as he pulled her back toward him, but it did her absolutely no good. He pulled her as if her entire one hundred and forty pounds were completely inconsequential.

When she was at the edge of the bed again, he pushed her body to the mattress and ran his hands down her back, stopping to squeeze her ass hard, causing Jody to let out a yelp.

"He may have said no fucking, but he didn't say anything about no touching."

Rodriguez's deep voice rumbled in her ear, and trepidation washed over her. She could think of all kinds of inappropriate touching one may or may not consider in the realm of fucking … and she didn't want Rodriguez to engage in any of them.

"Please don't hurt me," she begged, her voice muffled where her face pressed into the bed.

Her captor let out a dark chuckle and started to bind her hands with some kind of rope behind her back.

"As soon as he leaves us alone here, you can bet this sweet ass that I'm going to do whatever I want to you, and that most definitely means hurting you." He slipped a gag between her lips. "I'd rather be stuffing your mouth with something else, but I get the feeling you might be a biter," he said with another chuckle.

Rodriguez tied a knot in the material he used to gag her with a violent yank, ripping out some of her hairs in the process. Jody squeezed her eyes shut against the tears pricking her eyes and waited for whatever he would do to her next, knowing it was inevitable. She had never been a lay down and take it kind of woman, but in this case, it might be the only option she had if she wanted to get out of this alive. She'd already seen how much stronger and faster he was than her. There was no way she would be able to fight him off.

Warm, wet heat against her forearm surprised her, and her eyes popped wide open. It took her a moment before she realized it was his tongue gliding across the scratches from Plato on her arm. A burning sting emanated from where his saliva made contact with the open wounds and Jody shuddered.

"Mmmm, I knew you would taste good when I first caught a whiff of you," he whispered from behind her. "I can't wait to see what the rest of you tastes like."

He yanked on the waistband of her pajama pants and a rush of cool air kissed across her now-exposed backside. Jody squeezed her eyes shut again and tried to think of any place that wasn't here. Summers at the family cabin, swimming in the warm lakes. Camping up near Lake Superior. She was almost successful in drowning out the sensations of Rodriguez's warm breath across the back of her naked thighs, until his fingers trailed down between her cheeks to the edge of her underwear.

"Oh, this ass," Rodriguez groaned, grabbing both cheeks in his hands and squeezing so hard Jody knew there would be bruises there tomorrow.

Tears trickled down the side of her nose and a sob escaped from her, muffled by the gag in her mouth.

"What the fuck do you think you're doing?" a new voice Jody hadn't heard yet demanded. "You were supposed to tie her up and leave her here."

"Why are we listening to that fucker Micelli? He isn't one of us," Rodriguez bit out, his hands still perched firmly on her ass.

"Get your dick under control and get downstairs. He wants to go over strategy with us," the new voice rumbled.

"Fuck you, Kowalski. You know I've never been really good at following orders, why do you think I'm going to follow yours? Or that asshole's down there?" Rodriguez gave Jody another painful squeeze that made her whimper.

"If you don't follow Micelli's orders, you'll never get what you want. He's the only one who knows where that little bitch Nora is. We wouldn't even be in this situation if it wasn't for her," Kowalski spat.

"Fine, but when Micelli gets what he wants from her sister, I get to keep this one," Rodriguez demanded. "I mean, just look at that perfect ass."

"Let's go," Kowalski fumed. Jody could hear the barely concealed rage beneath the surface.

"Fine, fine, but don't go poaching what I've claimed," Rodriguez warned with a chuckle.

Rodriguez's presence behind her was suddenly gone, and the air in the room had somehow become less terrifying without him there. It was a moment before Jody heard any other movement in the room, and she was left to wonder if she was going to be abandoned with her pants down to her knees and her ass on display. A shuffle of footsteps toward her told her she wasn't alone like she thought. The guy Rodriguez called Kowalski was still in the room with her.

"Fuck," he whispered right before she felt a warm hand glide across her thigh and up over the swell of her ass.

Jody whimpered and nearly jumped a mile at the soft touch. His hand glided back down before he began pulling her pajama bottoms up. When her clothing was in place, he swung her feet up onto the bed and rolled her to her side so she faced the door. She couldn't get a good look at Kowalski's face in the dark room where the only illumination came from the glowing lights on the bedside table clock, but she assumed he was the third man who had stormed her house tonight.

"Get some sleep. If Rodriguez comes back, scream as loud as you can," he said. Then, as if waiting for the response he knew she would give, he paused before answering her unspoken words. "I'll hear you, even with the gag."

Jody strained to try to see him in the dark. There was something about his voice that was almost calm and comforting, but maybe that was just because he'd saved her—momentarily at least—from whatever plans Rodriguez had had for her. Resting his hand lightly on her shoulder, he gave it a squeeze before leaving the room. He pulled the door nearly closed behind him, leaving it open a crack.

The rumble of male voices drifted up the stairs through the crack in the door. One thing Jody learned when she first moved into this house was up in this room, she could hear just about *everything* that went on in the rest of the house. Sound echoed up the stairs, right into the master bedroom at the end of the hall—her room. It was this acoustical quality of the room that had allowed her to catch Plato before he destroyed a purse or a pair of shoes. Now, hopefully it would give her some kind of clue as to what sort of trouble her sister was in with these men.

CHAPTER THREE

Jody strained to hear the conversation from downstairs, but it wasn't quite like listening for her cat making mischief. She could hear they were talking, but she couldn't make out any of the words. In fact, she could barely decipher who was speaking, even though she was sure she would be able to recognize their voices anywhere after tonight.

After a few minutes of attempting to decode their murmured words, she gave up. Relaxing her head back onto the bed, she let out a sigh as the strain on her neck eased. She hadn't even realized how much effort it took to hold her head up at that angle.

Exhaustion hit her hard when her head made contact with the soft pillow. She wanted nothing more than to close her eyes and fall asleep, wishing when she woke in the morning she would find this all a bad nightmare. This couldn't be real. In movies, sure, but this kind of shit didn't happen in the real world. Especially not to her. She really had to stop watching thrillers right before bed.

She squeezed her eyes shut, trying to force away the events of the night.

It's not real. It's not real. It's not real, she recited in her head, hoping if she believed it enough it would go away. When she opened her eyes again, she was still bound on her bed in her dark room. Jody slammed her eyes shut again.

"It's not real. It's not real. It's not real," she chanted to herself through her gag. Maybe it would work if she said it aloud … you know, except for the part where having a gag in her mouth made it feel *really* real.

Cracking one eye open, Jody was once again met with the darkness of her room. A twitch of her wrist was accompanied by the burn of the rope against her skin, confirming this nightmare was indeed authentic. A broken sob escaped her and she pressed her face into her pillow to keep the men downstairs from hearing her break down. She wanted to put up a tough front, to channel the kickass heroines from her favorite movies and find a way to break free of her bindings and rescue herself. The only problem was, she was as far from kickass as one could get and she was scared shitless. She had no idea what kind of trouble her sister was in, and by extension what kind of trouble *she* was now it. It must be serious if there were men forcing their way into her house and keeping her prisoner.

Alicia, what have you done?

Jody didn't even know where Alicia was. She had to believe her sister was alive, otherwise it seemed to be wasted effort for these men to imprison her. She also had to believe Alicia didn't know they held her prisoner, otherwise she was certain Alicia would have already stormed the place to save her. Alicia had always been braver than her by miles. Jody sobbed into her gag, wishing she knew if her sister was all right.

"Shhhh," a voice came from the dark of Jody's room, but she couldn't tell from where exactly.

Holding her breath, she tried not to move a muscle as she pried her eyes open and peered into the darkness. Nothing, she could see absolutely nothing. Jody hadn't even heard him come into the room. Which one was it? Was it Rodriguez, back to finish what he started earlier?

The bed dipped down behind her and she tried to scramble toward the edge to get away, but a heavy hand on her shoulder held her to the mattress. Jody drew in a deep breath through her nose and screamed as loud as she could through the gag like Kowalski instructed her to.

"I'm right here," Kowalski's calming voice came from behind her, and Jody immediately ceased screaming. She hadn't realized until she stopped that she had been screaming his name.

Her breaths came in uneven, heaving gasps, and she closed her eyes in an attempt to keep the world from spinning. She was having a freaking panic attack.

"Take deep breaths," Kowalski soothed, his hand stroking up and down her arm.

Jody took in shaking breaths through her nose and breathed them out through the cloth shoved in her mouth. The repetitive motion of Kowalski's hand brought her frantic breathing down to a steady rhythm. Slowly, she opened her eyes and was relieved to find the room was no longer spinning like a runaway carousel.

"That's it, nice and calm," Kowalski's deep voice rumbled behind her. "Are you cold?" he asked when her tremors subsided.

Jody nodded. Kowalski's weight shifted from the bed, and then he placed a blanket over her. *Why is he being nice to me?* He broke into her house with the other two men and was keeping her prisoner. Was this some kind of good cop bad cop routine with Rodriguez?

Peeking over her shoulder, she hoped to get a glimpse of him in the dim light filtering in from the hallway now that the door was open. A cursory glance told her he was gorgeous. Even in the minimal light, Jody could see Kowalski was built like one of those ripped fitness models she had plastered all over her Facebook newsfeed. Longish hair hung down over his forehead, but she couldn't tell the color with the lighting. The same was true of his eyes; they appeared eerie in the gloom. An expression of sympathy—or was it pity?—marred his very handsome face and Jody had to avert her gaze. He was part of the reason she was in this situation, she didn't want to see him feeling sorry for her.

"Get some sleep." Coming around the bed so he faced her, he crouched down so his face was level with hers. She had to fight the urge to back away. He was too close. "No more crying, okay?" he whispered.

Jody also fought the urge to glare at him. How dare he tell her she couldn't cry after he'd turned her entire world upside down and dispelled any thoughts she had ever had that she was safe in her own home? She didn't know if she would ever feel safe again after all this.

"He likes it when they cry," Kowalski whispered again, his voice barely audible.

He? Does he mean Rodriguez? Jody's eyes opened wide with trepidation and comprehension. Kowalski nodded to her when he saw she understood and she nodded back. The last thing she wanted was another run-in with Rodriguez. She wouldn't be shedding anymore tears tonight if they were what would bring Rodriguez back.

"Everything's going to be okay, Jody. Once we get what your sister has, you can go back to living your life," he reassured, tucking a strand of hair behind her ear that had fallen over her face and had been tickling her nose. The gesture was too intimate, too familiar, and stunned her, but not enough for her to miss the uncertainty lacing his words.

Kowalski got up from where he crouched and made his way to the door, walking backward, his eyes never leaving her.

"Sleep," he commanded again before pulling the door closed all the way this time.

Jody heard the click of the latch and stared at the door for a moment. It was strange, the way he talked to her, the way he touched her spoke to a level of familiarity, but tonight was the first time she'd ever met him.

CHAPTER FOUR

The urgent need to pee woke Jody from a deep sleep. She tried to will the urge to empty her bladder away, but that had never worked before, so she couldn't see it working now. She moved to drag her exhausted body from the bed, but her arm was asleep. Tugging on her arms, Jody found she couldn't move them. Then when she tried to express her frustration with a curse, her words came out muffled.

Reality, along with her memories of last night, slammed into her like a ton of bricks. A part of her had still really believed it was all just some crazy manifestation of her love of high suspense movies into her dreams. The bright sunlight streaming from around the edges of her curtains told her it was definitely daylight, and the ropes still binding her wrists further cemented that this was not, in fact, a dream.

Panic grew in her chest and Jody counted out her breaths to keep them even so she didn't have a full-blown panic attack. Once her breathing was under control, the insistency of her bladder came into sharp focus. There was no way she could ignore it any longer.

Trying to kick the blanket off, Jody only succeeding in dislodging it from her lower half, then attempted to sit up without the assistance of her arms. The sheer effort it took really made her reconsider the ab workouts she'd been skipping lately. It took several tries before she was able to sit upright, and the relief her arms felt from the renewed blood flow was glorious. She didn't have time to enjoy it before the need to pee raised its ugly head again. She took a deep breath before swinging her legs over the side of the bed.

Okay, I can do this.

With feet touching the floor, Jody managed to get herself into a standing position. *Success.*

It was a little thing, but in light of everything that had happened in the last twelve hours or so, she'd take anything she could get at this point. Jody slowly tiptoed her way to the attached bathroom, shivering as her bare feet hit the cold tiles. When she got in front of the toilet, she realized she'd hit a snag. Dancing back and forth from one foot to the other, she squeezed her thighs together, looking like a toddler doing a potty dance. This was ridiculous. She was sure she *looked* ridiculous. How the hell was she going to do this with her hands tied behind her back? One hand, sure, she'd had to do that when she'd sprained her wrist in high school, but *both* hands? That was an *entirely* different story.

Balancing on one foot, she managed to open the lid with the other. She celebrated with a grin, a minor and short-lived victory to be sure. Using her bound hands, she worked her pajama pants and underwear down her thighs an inch at a time and plopped down on the seat just as the first drops escaped without her permission. Jody let out a groan of relief as she emptied the contents of her bladder into the toilet. She had no idea how she was going to wipe and there was almost no chance of being able to wash her hands. These were the logistical things they never showed in the movies, and she definitely wished they had so she had something to reference.

After contemplating the scenario, she managed to pull some paper from the roll, set it on the edge of the toilet seat and sit on it. Another success! One step at a time. Anything to keep her mind off the reason her hands were tied in the first place.

When she stood, her pants and underwear slipped down her legs to her ankles. *Really?* Throwing her head back, Jody squeezed her eyes shut to keep from losing it and breaking down into tears. This was some kind of horrific comedy of errors where just about everything that could go wrong *was* going wrong. Well, except she didn't pee the bed. That had to count for something, right?

Taking a deep, calming breath and letting it out noisily through her gagged mouth, Jody reopened her eyes and stared at the cloth pooled around her ankles. *I can do this, I can totally do this.*

Crouching down awkwardly, she grabbed for the waistband of her pants. She dropped it on the first try, but succeeded on the second. Now that she had them, she had no idea how she was going to get them up. Jody thought for a brief, humiliating moment about calling for Kowalski to help her, but dismissed that almost before it had a chance to finish playing out in her mind. Yeah. No. That wasn't going to happen. It would be just her luck Rodriguez would come instead and take her complete lack of ass covering as an invitation. Just the thought of his hands on her again gave her a renewed sense of determination.

Using a combination of very unattractive grunting and tugging, along with some rather lewd movements of her hips, Jody managed to get her pants—with her underwear trapped somewhere in the middle, but she could deal with them later—up over her knees. Alternating lifting one knee and then the other while kneeling on the floor, she finally pulled the waistband up over her ass to rest where it belonged.

Kneeling on the tile for a moment, out of breath, Jody tried to ignore the uncomfortable feeling of her underwear's waistband sitting askew across the underside of her butt-cheeks. She decided she would just ignore it until she got back to the bed; maybe she could deal with it better while lying down. When she felt she'd caught her breath, she wobbled to her feet again and gazed longingly at the sink, the nurse in her wishing desperately to wash her hands. There was no way she didn't get pee on her hands *somewhere* with all that *Cirque du Soleil* nonsense she had to do just to get her pants up. Her eyes moved from the shiny faucet to the equally shiny pair of scissor she left there after she violated the first rule of haircare yesterday and trimmed her own hair.

The barest hint of a creak in the floor snapped her gaze from the scissors up to the mirror to find a man standing behind her. Jody startled, but then was mesmerized by the reflection. She studied him for a moment, taking in a devastatingly handsome, though stoic, face. His dark hair was shorn short, and the width of his shoulders, clothed in a T-shirt, betrayed alarming strength. Her gaze moved back up from his powerful muscles to where his mouth was set in a cruel smirk.

"What are you doing out of bed?" he asked, Jody's eyes riveted on the reflection of his mouth as he spoke.

With his first word, Jody's entire body broke into a cold sweat, sheer terror flooding her system. She drew in a shaking breath and felt her body quake. Though she hadn't seen Rodriquez last night, she would definitely never forget the sound of his voice.

CHAPTER FIVE

Suppressing a sob, Jody's gaze drifted from those lips to the dark pits of his eyes. They were startlingly black, and she was unable to decipher where the pupil ended and the iris began. It was like looking into a dark void threatening to swallow her whole. There was no pity there like she saw in Kowalski's eyes last night when he brushed her hair from her face. Rodriguez's eyes were filled with malice and dark intent.

"I asked you a question," Rodriguez demanded, grabbing Jody's hair and wrenching her head around so she faced him in the flesh instead of his reflection.

Jody bit the inside of her cheek to keep a cry from escaping, remembering Kowalski's words from last night about Rodriguez's affinity for his victims' tears. He wetted his lips while his eyes roamed over her face. She couldn't hold back the whimper that escaped when his predatory gaze met hers again.

"Music to my ears," he whispered, and his eyes slid down to her neck. "I love the way your heart races when I'm around," he chuckled, then licked along the spot on her neck where her pulse beat a rapid staccato.

Near to hyperventilating now, Jody tried to draw enough oxygen into her lungs around the rag still gagging her. Rodriguez's teeth scraped along the same spot he'd just licked, nipping at the delicate skin there. Another terrified whimper escaped from her, and Rodriguez let out a dark chuckle.

"Just one little taste," he whispered, "you tasted so good last night."

Rodriguez's teeth glided along her neck again and his grip tightened on her hair. His other arm snaked around to roughly pull her body flush with his, squeezing the air from her. He held on tightly. So tightly Jody couldn't pull in a breath. She struggled, trying to loosen his grip, but he only constricted more. Using the little breath she could pull in, Jody screamed for him to stop, but the words came out a muffled cry around the gag.

Pounding footsteps sounded on the stairs, and Rodriguez spun Jody out of his grip so fast, the room spun. He steadied her with a hand clasping the back of her neck.

"What the fuck do you think you're doing?" Kowalski's voice exploded before he even burst into the room.

"Micelli wants her downstairs," Rodriguez sneered.

"You know you're not supposed to touch her," Kowalski accused, his nostrils flaring and his chest rising and falling with rapid breaths.

Rodriguez just laughed at him. "We'll see about that."

Kowalski's eyes narrowed and he glowered at Rodriguez. Jody was taken aback at how menacing he looked, threat pouring off him to rival Rodriguez.

Rodriquez yanked on her arms and pushed past Kowalski, dragging her from the room. She looked over her shoulder back to Kowalski, begging him with her eyes not to leave her alone with Rodriguez again. Kowalski's footsteps followed quietly behind them and Jody felt at least some relief he would be there. She knew it was ludicrous to feel safe with one of her captors, but right now, she would take the lesser of the two evils. Where Rodriguez seemed to want to cause her harm, Kowalski gave the impression he would protect her from it.

When they got to the top of the stairs, Rodriguez dragged her down by her arm. Jody stumbled with each step, having no ability to catch herself. Halfway down, he stopped and roughly threw her over his shoulder with an annoyed huff. Each jolting step jammed his shoulder into her stomach and by the time they reached the living room, she wanted to vomit. She probably would have if there had been anything *to* vomit.

Rodriguez dumped her unceremoniously onto the floor at the feet of another man. This one Jody recognized from last night. He was the one who knocked on her door and gave the orders. Kowalski and Rodriguez called him Micelli.

"Where's your phone?" he demanded without preamble.

Jody didn't know how he expected her to answer. She could neither speak nor point her answer. Apparently seeing this flaw in his interrogation, he nodded over to Kowalski.

"Take off the gag," Micelli ordered.

Kowalski came behind her and untied the piece of fabric they used as a gag. His touch was gentle, yet she couldn't help but wince when the little hairs at the back of her neck were pulled. When the cloth dropped away, Jody breathed out a sigh of relief and licked across her poor parched lips.

"Well, where is it?" Micelli demanded impatiently.

"The couch," Jody answered, puzzled by the question and further puzzled by the fact they hadn't seen it sitting there. She'd left it on the arm when she had gotten up to answer their knock last night.

"Get it," Micelli ordered Rodriguez, who stood closest to the couch.

It only took Rodriguez two strides before he reached the piece of furniture. From this vantage point, Jody could see all of him now, and the sight was terrifying. The man was *huge* all over. Her gaze drifted over to Kowalski, who was really not much smaller. Where the hell did these guys come from?

"It's not here," Rodriguez announced after surveying the area.

Sharp pain exploded in Jody's scalp where Micelli gripped her hair and yanked her head back so she faced him.

"Ow!" Jody cried out, her eyes welling with tears.

"It's not there, where is it?" Micelli demanded, shaking her hair like she was some misbehaving dog.

"I-I don't know. Maybe it fell beneath or between the cushions?" she gasped when he started to lift her by her hair.

Micelli held her in position while Rodriguez rifled through the cushions. Jody breathed a small sigh of relief when he produced the phone from within the upholstery. Rodriguez tossed the phone to Micelli and he dropped his hold on her hair to catch it. Swiping his fingers across the screen, he paused.

"What's the password?" he demanded, his eyes now boring into hers.

Jody's brain stopped for a minute. It was ridiculous, but it was one of those things she could barely remember the password unless she was typing it in.

"Um nine five one two," she blurted out when he took a menacing step toward her.

He stopped half a foot from her and punched in the code, then walked away and sat casually on the couch, crossing his ankle over one knee. A nod of silent communication passed between him and Rodriguez, and suddenly Rodriguez was standing in front of where she knelt on the floor.

"I like you in this position, but we'll save that for later," he said with a suggestive lift of his eyebrows. Kowalski let out a soft growl from behind her.

Rodriguez took up the grip on her hair where Micelli dropped it earlier, and pulled on it until tears came to her eyes. Jody tried to keep from giving him the satisfaction of crying out.

"Stand the fuck up!" he yelled.

Jody scrambled to push up to her feet without the aid of her hands, but found it was a lot more difficult than she anticipated. When she'd almost gotten all the way to standing, her foot slipped on the hem of her pajama pants and she went tumbling to the floor, leaving strands of her hair in Rodriguez's hands.

Micelli sighed in boredom and shook his head from the couch. Gentle hands helped her to her feet so she stood facing Rodriguez. Anger flared in her, not at the man who'd ripped out her hair, but at the one with the caring touch who helped her. How could he be nice to her one moment, but watch them hurt her the next?

Gripping her chin in his big hand, Rodriguez tilted her face up to him. The gesture wrenched her head back to look up at him. If she had to guess, she would have to say he was at least a foot taller than her five foot four inches. His eyes raked over her face again, much like they had in the bathroom upstairs. The blatant appraisal giving her the chills.

"So fucking beautiful," he complimented, then finished with, "It's too bad we're going to have to fuck up that pretty face."

Jody was stunned for a minute, not understanding what was happening until his grip left her chin and the same hand came back to strike her across the cheek. The impact of the blow threw her to the floor. Pain exploded across her cheekbone and a keening wail she'd never heard come out of her own mouth before sounded from her lips.

"What the fuck?" Kowalski shouted, jumping between her and Rodriguez. "I thought you said you weren't going to hurt her?" he threw the accusation over to Micelli.

Micelli shrugged and stood from the couch. "We need a little incentive for her sister. She's a tough one, your sister," Micelli told Jody. "You know, I offered her a job and she turned it down. I tried to convince her last night to change her mind, but she somehow got away and one of my guys is also missing … presumed dead."

Alicia *killed* someone?

He tsked at her when he must have seen the horrified expression on her face. "No," he sighed. "Endre's man took care of that. Then we lost track of her. Weeks of tracking her movements and trying to bring her around, and now we can't even find her!" He slammed his fist down on the arm of the couch where he'd repositioned himself. "We'll find her soon enough though, we've been keeping an eye on you to use as leverage in case she refused to cooperate. And if I've learned anything about your sister, it's that she would do almost anything for you, wouldn't she?" he guessed with smile.

Jody had no idea who Endre was, but he sounded like another dangerous man she didn't want to know. And they had been watching *her*? For how long? What was this? Some kind of gang war or something? She bit her tongue so she didn't ask the questions aloud. She didn't want to risk drawing their attention to the fact she was still there and silently cataloging any information she could pick up from the conversation. She was pretty damned sure they would throw her back into her room—or worse—if they realized she was actually paying attention.

An electronic ping sounded from in Micelli's direction and Jody held her breath. Pulling a phone out of his jacket pocket, Micelli looked at it. A grin spread across his face and he glanced up at Rodriguez.

"Alicia just arrived home," Micelli announced. "I thought for sure they'd keep her at the lab. She knows the location," he mumbled to himself while stroking one hand over his chin, deep in thought. "Change of plans, boys. Rodriguez, you head over to her place. You're going to scare her ... only scare, don't injure her beyond repair. I want her running back to the protection of Endre's lab. She's going to help them instead of us starting from scratch." Micelli's gaze turned to Jody. "Don't worry, you've still got a part to play. We're going to hang on to you to make sure big sister does what she's told."

Micelli nodded another order in that silent language she didn't understand to Rodriguez. His fist came flying at her and connected with her mouth, slamming her head into the floor. A burst of pain emanated from where her tooth cut into her lip and coppery liquid filled her mouth almost instantly.

"Fuck!" she cried out, squeezing her eyes shut against the pain.

"Smile pretty, sweetheart," Micelli encouraged with a vile grin and snapped a picture of her lying on the floor with her phone. That grin stayed plastered to his face while he tapped on the phone. "Get going," he ordered Rodriguez without looking up.

CHAPTER SIX

Micelli sat on the couch staring at her in silence for nearly fifteen minutes, as best as Jody could tell. It was an uncomfortable appraisal, cold and calculating as if he was mapping out the next move in a game of chess where she was but a pawn. She was glad it wasn't one of the hungry looks Rodriguez had been giving her. Keeping her face pressed against the floor, Jody hid behind the locks of hair that fell over her eyes, focusing on the irregular patterns in the hardwood floor just beyond the rug. It kept her mind off the throbbing pain in her face where she'd been struck, but it didn't keep her mind from wandering to what Micelli had said about Vampires. Was it all just the ravings of a madman? Or was there really some hidden world of mythical creatures she was thrust into?

Movement in front of her brought Jody's attention to Micelli once more. He flipped her phone and glanced at the time before tapping on the screen. A few movements later, and he brought her phone up to his ear and waited. After a moment, Jody watched the corners of his mouth turn up into a smile. She imagined if his smile didn't have the edge of cruelty, she might have thought him attractive. Just like Rodriguez. Just like Kowalski. He may not have been the one hurting her, but he stood by and let it happen, and that told her all she needed to know about what kind of man he was. Not a good one, despite his attempts to comfort her and convince her otherwise.

"Ms. Matthews, good morning to you, too," Micelli suddenly chuckled, his voice too loud breaking into the silence which had enveloped the room over the past quarter of an hour.

Jody's breath hitched at the sound of her name. And her sister's.

"I suppose I can't expect you to recognize my voice in your distressed state. Perhaps you remember our conversation last week?" he asked in a soothing tone.

Micelli silently laughed to himself while Alicia answered, then turned his gaze to where Jody was still sprawled on the floor. She hadn't bothered to attempt to get up after Rodriguez hit her, seeing as it was a feat of acrobatics to do anything with her hands tied behind her back.

"You did," he said, answering her sister on the phone, his eyes never leaving Jody, "and, I told you I wouldn't take no for an answer. Consider this me increasing your incentive for working for me. You have a message to view." His voice held an edge of warning Jody knew even Alicia wouldn't miss through the phone.

"Oh, I think you do. You're a smart woman, Ms. Matthews, which is precisely why I wanted you to join my team. But, since I assume you are feeling out of sorts this morning from your ordeal last night, I will spell it out for you. If you want your sister to remain unharmed, you will work for me," he stated, his voice a warning to Alicia and the expression on his face a warning to Jody.

"You'll still work for me, but in a different capacity. It will require a bit of acting skills, do you think you can do that? To save your sister?" he mocked.

Jody was doomed. Alicia had never been able to lie to save her soul; she always got busted when they were kids. Not that Jody's acting skills were any better, but right now, her life wasn't depending on them. She had to believe Alicia would do everything she could to save her.

"I knew I could count on you," he said gleefully. "I want you to go back to the Vampire's lab. I want you to tell them you were attacked in your home. Endre's new man will surely want to keep you safe and insist you stay with them … he seems rather protective of you. Then, I want you to offer up your skills, the skills you denied my use of, to help them in their research."

Wait. More talk of Vampires? What? Listening raptly to the lunacy coming from Micelli, Jody wondered exactly how much her sister was freaking out right about now.

Micelli let out a bored sigh. "Ms. Matthews, it is getting tedious explaining every detail to you. You will infiltrate their lab, assist them—I want them to succeed in their endeavor—and then you will report their results to me. Your sister's life depends on your ability to make a convincing performance, remember that," Micelli warned.

A dark look passed over his face as he listened. Jody wished he'd put it on speaker so she could hear Alicia's voice. It was quite possible it might be the last time she ever would.

"You are in no position to make demands, it would seem you forget I hold all the cards here. As for your sister's welfare, that depends on you. I will keep her from further harm as long as you hold up your end of the bargain. I want a daily update on their progress as well as any other tidbits you can provide about their security or anything else you deem of relevance that might assist me," he told her.

A pause.

"At your sister's number. I'll be holding onto her phone for the time being," he said, giving Jody a smile. "I think it's time you were on your way. I've also sent along one of my associates to lend credibility to the story you will tell the Vampires. We'll be in touch, Ms. Matthews." Micelli ended the call.

"If you're going to keep her safe, what do you want to do about Rodriguez?" Kowalski asked, crossing his arms over his chest and staring down Micelli.

Micelli chuckled. "Nothing. I don't give a shit what happens to her, just as long as she stays alive. Just don't give her any blood. I don't want her turning into a fucking parasite," Micelli sneered with disdain.

"Blood?" Jody couldn't help herself from asking.

Both pairs of eyes landed on her and she suddenly wished she'd kept her mouth shut.

"That's right, sweetheart. Blood. I bet it would interest you to know your knight in shining armor here is a Vampire," Micelli informed with an evil laugh.

"Like, a real Vampire?" she asked slowly, wondering if there was some kind of metaphor she was missing that might explain the utter insanity of the statement. Maybe it was a code word they used for a rival gang? The mention of blood *was* rather disconcerting though.

"Yes, like a real Vampire. As in, he drinks blood to stay alive," Micelli chortled, his laugh increasing in volume as he took in the look of embarrassment on Kowalski's face.

"Are you one too?" she couldn't help herself from asking, her voice wavering.

"Fuck no. My kind has been hunting his kind for thousands of years. That's enough questions. Get her back up to her room," Micelli barked at Kowalski.

Jody shrank back from Kowalski when he reached for her, and she could have sworn she saw hurt flash across his face before he replaced it with a cold mask of indifference. Hauling her to her feet, Kowalski pushed her out the room and back up the stairs. She stumbled up them, slipping and hitting her shoulder as she neared the top. Who knew how much she relied on her arms to keep her balance on stairs? At least they seemed to decide she no longer needed to be gagged.

"Make sure you gag her, I don't want to hear any more questions out of that pretty mouth," Micelli yelled from the living room.

Jody nearly groaned aloud. Apparently her thoughts about being gagged were a bit premature.

"I'm going to see Jaqueline. And, Kowalski?" Micelli said, pausing for Kowalski to answer. When he didn't, Micelli continued, his voice pitching low and threatening, "That one better still be here when I get back, or I will hunt you down and take your head so fast it won't have time to spin."

A shiver ran through Jody at the warning in his tone that bade all who heard it to take heed and obey. All the hopeful thoughts she had about Kowalski possibly helping her escape fled her brain.

CHAPTER SEVEN

Kowalski pushed her through the bedroom door and closed it behind them. Jody stood still, waiting for him to gag her. She resigned herself to the idea now that she knew what he was. The last thing she wanted was to give him a reason to bite her. He brushed past her and the hammering of her heart kicked up, was he going to hurt her *now*?

"I'm not going to hurt you, Jody." Sitting down on the bed in front of her, he scrubbed his hands down his face.

"Aren't you going to gag me?" she whispered in confusion.

"No," his muffled voice came through his hands.

"Are you going to bite me?" Jody asked, trepidation dancing across her skin.

Lifting his face from his hands, Kowalski shook his head at her, a note of sadness in it. "No," he replied, then let out a huff before laughing to himself.

Jody watched whatever monologue was happening in his head play across his face, where he went from incredulous to sad to angry. The angry part scared her and she took a step back.

"He said that on purpose so you'd be just as scared of me as you are of Rodriguez," Kowalski said aloud, shaking his head again.

"So, you're not one? A Vampire, I mean?" she questioned, hoping maybe the guy sitting on her bed wasn't really some deadly predator.

"No, I am a," he paused, "Vampire, but I'm not like Rodriguez."

"Rodriguez isn't a Vampire?" Jody asked, wondering if maybe he was something else entirely. It seemed Micelli was ... he did say his 'kind,'? Maybe he was a werewolf. Oh God, were werewolves real, too?

"Yes, he is a Vampire. I just meant I'm not the same kind of *person,*" Kowalski answered, his eyes watching her intently.

If she thought back to her two very terrifying interactions with Rodriguez, Jody would see the truth. Today he had been licking her neck over her carotid and talking about having a taste. The thought made her shudder. Yesterday, he licked across her scrapes from Plato.

Plato!

"Did you guys hurt Plato?" Jody asked, her voice coming out in a tremor at the thought of them torturing her poor fur baby.

"Plato?" Kowalski startled with confusion, eyeing her warily.

Jody was sure he thought she'd gone off the deep end. And why not? She'd just learned Vampires were real and there was one sitting on her bed and a sadistic one who really wanted to hurt her. She didn't doubt given the next opportunity to be alone with her without supervision, he would.

"My cat," Jody replied by way of explanation.

"No, we didn't hurt your cat." Sighing, Kowalski hung his head. The dejected expression on his face made her feel almost ... bad.

"What's wrong?" she couldn't help herself from asking. What a stupid question to ask. *Everything* was wrong here.

Kowalski looked up at her and chuckled. "This is so fucked up."

Jody could only nod in response. This *was* pretty fucked up. Vampires. What the hell?

"I thought if I finally got a chance to talk to you, you'd see I'm not like them. And now you think I'm a monster." He gritted his teeth. "I'm *not* a monster. Not like him," Kowalski spit out emphatically.

Jody stared at him with wide eyes. Now who was the one sounding all kinds of crazy?

"Finally?" she inquired quietly, trying to wrap her head around the implications of his statement. "Wait, that guy said someone had been watching me. *You?*"

"Yeah. Me. For *weeks*," Kowalski admitted, shaking his head, then stood up and came toward her.

"Like, *here?*" she choked out, thinking about how that could mean he'd seen more of her than any other man had since her boyfriend from a year and a half ago. She took a step back and he took another forward, getting entirely too close.

"At home, at work, you name it. Anywhere you went, I followed," he acknowledged quietly, a manic kind of glint in his eyes.

"That's really creepy," she whispered. "And you thought if you talked to me … what?"

"You know, I tried to talk to you once at the coffee shop. The one in the hospital you go to every day before your shift starts?" he recalled, taking another step forward and pushing her another step back. "You barely even glanced at me."

Jody detected a hint of pain in the words, but didn't respond. She didn't know *how* to respond to that. He'd been stalking her and now he seemed to have some kind of expectation. It explained why he acted so familiar with her. He believed he knew her.

"I thought if I could convince you I was one of the good guys, you'd see I took on the job watching you so it wouldn't be Rodriguez. He's a sadistic fuck, and … well, you've already seen how he is," Kowalski explained, shaking his head and laughing, the sound on the edge of madness.

Jody took another step away, but her back pressed against the closed door and there was nowhere left to go. Kowalski placed both hands on the door on either side of her shoulders, trapping her in on all sides. Panic started to rise in her chest. At least with Rodriguez she had an idea of what he wanted from her; with Kowalski, she was at a loss. That unknown factor made him even more dangerous than Rodriguez right now.

Kowalski leaned forward and closed his eyes before inhaling deeply near her neck. "Fuck, you smell good. I knew you would." His breath fanned over her face.

Jody held back a whimper as he buried his face in her neck.

"You're scared of me," he stated, then pulled back so he met her terrified gaze. His hand came up to cup her cheek and his touch no longer felt comforting as it did before. Now it felt *wrong*. "It wasn't supposed to happen this way!" he yelled suddenly, slamming his hand against the door and making her jump. "The plan was simple: Micelli was supposed to get your sister to work for him and whip up the cure. Then we were all supposed to take it. You were just a contingency, you weren't supposed to be in the middle of everything."

Cure. Jody latched onto the one word, and decided to try a different tactic. She needed to get him talking and thinking about something else. Anything else.

"Cure for what? Vampires? You want to be human?" Jody pressed, trying to inject curiosity into her voice so he wouldn't hear her fear. It seemed to agitate him when she showed she was afraid of him.

"Yes, I was supposed to be human when I met you the first time. But your sister ruined it all," he shouted, slamming his hand on the door again, much too close to her head.

The sound and the vibration made her flinch and she squeezed her eyes closed.

"Do you think I'm going to hurt you, Jody?" he demanded, then his voice went soft again. "I would never. I won't let anyone hurt you. He can't have you, you're mine. I love you."

Jody couldn't miss the sheer possessiveness in his tone and it terrified her.

"Did you hear me? I. Love. You." He punctuated his words with kisses to her cheeks and then her lips.

She held back sobs when his lips landed on her. They felt just as vile as his violation into her life. A shudder ran through her and a sob she'd been holding back finally escaped her mouth. How could she have thought he would be the one to keep her safe throughout all this? He was the most dangerous of the three of them.

CHAPTER EIGHT

"Don't you have anything to say?" Kowalski's pleading voice broke through Jody's terrified thoughts.

Opening her eyes, Jody gaped at him. What did he expect her to say? Did he expect her to tell her she loved him back? She didn't know him. He was a Vampire. He broke into her house, tied her up, and stood by while Rodriguez hit her.

"Do you think I'm a monster?" he implored, obviously asking her to tell him the opposite.

What was she supposed to say to that?

"Am I a monster?" he demanded, gripping her chin in his hand in a way that wouldn't be described as gentle.

Jody still didn't answer, her mouth opening and closing like a fish. Her brain was frozen, not knowing which answer the volatile Vampire wanted. She didn't want to think what he was capable of if she gave him the *wrong* one. She was entirely at the mercy of his emotions, and they didn't look to be terribly stable right now.

"Answer me," Kowalski growled, and Jody could see fangs elongate.

"No," she lied quickly, her terrified gaze riveted on the fangs. He really was a Vampire. He really *was* a monster.

"Liar!" he roared, spittle hitting her cheek. "I didn't think you were a liar. You're not supposed to be a liar. Of course you think I am a monster. I drink blood."

Jody whimpered and closed her eyes shut tight when he came closer. His breath fanned over her neck, over the same spot where Rodriguez had licked her. Over the spot she knew he wanted to bite her with those vicious fangs.

"I want your blood. It's mine. *You're* mine, do you understand me, Jody?" he whispered dangerously in her ear. "He doesn't get you. Not even a taste. I didn't want this for us. I didn't want to be this."

Entire body quaking, Jody waited for him to bite her. Kowalski's breaths came in warm puffs across her skin, but she still felt as cold as if she stood outside in the Minnesota winter.

"You know I'm just trying to protect you, right? I'm trying to protect what's mine." Kowalski was sounding more desperate by the second.

"Yes," she managed to whisper out the lie.

The last thing she wanted was to anger him more, and she hoped she could placate him enough to loosen the grip he had on her. It was almost too much to hope he would leave her in her room unscathed.

"From him. I'm protecting you from him. You have no idea what he's capable of. I would never hurt you like he would. Do you believe me?" the Vampire pleaded, his hand moving from her face to grip her shoulder. She winced as his other hand gripped equally hard on her other shoulder and he gave her a small shake, banging her head on the door.

Jody nodded. What the hell was she going to do? There was no precedent for this, she didn't know how to talk to someone as unhinged as Kowalski had become. There were times at the hospital when she had to deal with patients who were on the edge, but none of them were ever quite as far gone as he was now. And none of them chose her as the object of their agitation.

"We're leaving," he announced suddenly, squeezing her shoulders. "That's the only way to make sure he doesn't take you from me. We have to go."

Kowalski's body no longer trapped her against the door and Jody slid to the floor. From her perch against the door, she watched helplessly as he pulled a bag from her closet and began shoving clothing inside it with no rhyme or reason. He ripped tank tops from their hangers; he shoved shorts and socks and dresses into the bag. Every movement was frantic and disjointed. Unstable.

Leaving with Kowalski would be trading one form of captivity for another. His passionate declarations of possession scared the living daylights out of Jody. He could take her from this house, far away from the harm Micelli and Rodriguez might inflict upon her, but at least Alicia knew where she was. If he took her from here, no one would ever find her.

Jody couldn't leave with him. She had to find a way to make him stay, to stall for more time. Micelli may not have intentions of keeping her whole, but he had no desire to consume her like Kowalski did. His brand of consumption didn't include only her blood, but the whole of her. He wanted every last piece of her, and she could see he intended to take them from her bit by bit. She couldn't let him.

"Kowalski?" Jody coaxed quietly, but he didn't slow from rifling through her clothes. "Kowalski!" she demanded louder, and he paused to look at her where she sat huddled on the floor. "What about my sister?"

"Your sister?" he asked, puzzled. "We can't bring her with us. I can't get her out of the lab," he stated, shaking his head.

"Won't they hurt her?" she questioned, then added for good measure, trying to make sure it didn't come off too strong, "I don't know what I'd do if she got hurt."

A sob rent from her chest, one Jody didn't even have to fake. Imagining her life without her sister splintered her heart.

"Hey," Kowalski soothed, dropping the clothing he held and came to her.

Kneeling in front of her, he took Jody's face in his hands gently—much more gently than when his hands were on her earlier. The pads of his thumbs wiped away the tears from her eyes and the gesture made her cry harder. It was that tender action every woman fantasizes her loving partner would perform when she cries, and now it was sullied by the deranged Vampire before her.

"They're not going to hurt her," he reassured. "Is there anything you would like to take with us when we go?"

Jody shook her head, attempting to stifle her tears. She really was no good at manipulation. She was pretty sure she made things worse asking about Alicia's fate. Now he wanted to take her away more than ever.

"I-I have to pee," Jody choked out through her tears.

That wasn't part of her manipulation; she really did have to pee. But she also hoped for a few moments to gather her thoughts and her wits. Maybe even with her hands free. That last hope might be too much to ask for. He was clearly wary of her evading him, so she didn't think he'd relent to removing her bonds.

"Of course," Kowalski sighed, helping her to her feet and ushering her to the bathroom.

"Um," she started, biting her lip with uncertainty, "can you untie me?"

She had to ask. He might get angry or suspicious and say no, but she wouldn't know if she didn't ask. He stared at her for a moment, narrowing his eyes and searching for the ruse.

"It was hard to wipe last time," Jody finally whispered, hanging her head in shame.

Kowalski sighed before he stepped behind her and untied the knots. When the cording fell away, Jody winced as blood rushed into her fingers, feeling like a million little stabbing needles. Flexing her hands, she tried to speed up the flow of blood, hoping it would chase away the pins and needles.

"Thank you," she offered, giving him a forced smile.

Nodding, he turned back to the bag and continued to shove clothing into it.

"Hurry, we leave soon," he ordered without looking at her.

Jody didn't acknowledge his statement and instead made her way into the bathroom. Sitting heavily on the toilet, she tried to come up with a plan. Her eyes went to the lock on the door. She could lock it and try to squeeze out the small window. But the door was one of those cheap, hollow core ones and wouldn't stop someone of Kowalski's size even without the Vampire strength. Forget the fact she was up on the second floor and had no idea how she would get to the ground without jumping. Into the snow no less. Without a coat. Without boots. Yeah, she wouldn't make it very far. Her eyes scanned the ugly wallpaper on the wall she hadn't yet had time to rip off, hoping its hideous pattern would give her a clue on what she should do. It provided no such inspiration. The scissors on the vanity did, though.

A light tapping on the door broke her gaze from the scissors.

"We have to go," Kowalski urged, his voice harried.

"Almost done," she croaked out.

Jody wiped and washed her hands methodically, her eyes never leaving the scissors. She didn't know anything about Vampires in real life, and she didn't know what of the information she knew from books and movies was real. Would he bleed if she stabbed him? Would she be able to kill him with the scissors? Where would she have to stab him to kill him? If he were a human man, she would aim for the throat, in that same spot both Vampires seemed to have been so fond of on her neck.

As she shut off the water and began to dry her hands, the door swung open, and Kowalski stood waiting with her bag slung over his shoulder. His stance was imposing and gave him a commanding presence. If circumstances were different, if he hadn't been a Vampire who broke into her home and proved himself mentally unstable, she thought she might find herself attracted to him.

"Let's go," he commanded, holding out his hand for her to take.

CHAPTER NINE

Jody warily placed her hand in Kowalski's, feeling like she just signed her death warrant. He pulled her to her bedroom door. Every step required extreme effort not to rip her hand from his.

Kowalski grasped the doorknob and paused. Cocking his head to the side, he listened. Pulling his hand back from the door suddenly, he turned to her, indecision warring in his eyes. He ran his teeth over his bottom lip, as if deep in thought, and Jody couldn't help but follow the movement of his mouth, watching for any sign of those lethal fangs.

"We're out of time," Kowalski whispered, and Jody's gaze snapped up to his eyes.

"What does that mean?" she asked, but he was already tossing the packed bag back into the closet and pulling her toward the bed.

When he picked up the rope from the floor, Jody tried to pull her hand out of his grip, but he wouldn't let go.

"What's happening?'" Jody demanded, tugging on her hand frantically.

On one hand, she seemed to have gotten her hopes answered about not leaving with him, but on the other, she really didn't want to be tied up again.

Kowalski's expression was apologetic as he whipped her around and pressed her into the bed. The feeling of being pressed into her mattress like Rodriguez had done sent her into a panic. *What's happening?* The burn of the rope around her wrists again brought tears to her eyes.

"Rodriguez is back, and there's no way we could have made it out of here before he arrived. I'm sorry, Jo," Kowalski apologized in her ear, barely above a whisper. "I won't win if it comes to a fight."

Jody tried to yank her arms from his grasp before he pulled the rope tight, but he was too strong. She hated that he called her by her nickname reserved for family and friends. Kowalski was neither.

"Stop fighting, you're going to hurt yourself," he warned, flipping her body onto the bed with so little effort it was terrifying. His display of strength was a sobering reminder of just how helpless she was in this scenario.

When Kowalski reached for her foot, she kicked out at him, but his hand was a blur as he caught her foot before she could even come close to connecting with any part of his body. He forced her leg down to the bed next to her other one and wrapped rope around her ankles. He knotted it tightly while she screamed obscenities at him.

"You fucking lied to me! You said you were going to protect me! You're right, you are a monster! You sick f—" Jody screamed at him before her words were cut off when a piece of cloth was shoved in her mouth and another was wrapped around her head to keep it in place.

Anger laced Kowalski's features when he looked down at her.

"I am not a monster and I didn't lie. I will get you out of here, but it's too much of a risk to do it right now. If he fought me and he won, you would be his. I can't let that happen. You're mine!" he whispered fiercely, each word bringing him closer to her face.

Jody stared daggers at him, wishing very much for the phrase "if looks could kill" to be a truth. Part of her was relieved she wouldn't be dragged out into the wide world with only the psychopath as her company, but the other part of her was pissed at how helpless she was lying bound on her bed – again.

"I'll be back in a few hours with some food. Try to be quiet and don't draw attention to yourself," he warned before striding to the door.

Jody hurled muffled obscenities at his back as he exited her room and pulled the door shut behind him. What the hell was she going to do now? She was tied up on her bed and he said it would be *hours* before he came back for her.

A few hours later—or so Jody guessed since she couldn't see her clock—she was no closer to coming up with an escape plan. Her wrists and her ankles hurt, and things were starting to go numb. And she had to pee … again. Of course she had to pee. If Kowalski had left her legs untied, she could have gone to the bathroom by herself. It wasn't like she'd mastered the art of peeing with her hands tied behind her back, but she managed it last time, hadn't she?

Jody wondered if Kowalski would hear her and take her to the bathroom if she screamed for him. She was sure someone would come, she just didn't want it to be Rodriguez or Micelli. Although, she wasn't sure she wanted Kowalski either. Maybe a few hours away from her had settled him down a bit. Either way, she was faced once again with choices which were no better than the other: pee her bed and lay in it for God knows how long, or call for the deranged Vampire who claimed he was in love with her to bring her to the toilet. Neither were ideal options. But this wasn't one of those times when not choosing was a choice, because if she didn't choose, her bladder would just pick the first option and there would be nothing she could do about it. She wasn't to the point of exploding yet, but definitely needing to go enough that it was uncomfortable and the only thing she would be able to think about until someone came to her rescue. Rescue being a relative term in this case.

Fifteen minutes later, there were still no signs of Kowalski coming to bring her some food, and she was getting desperate. The only way she knew it had been that long was because she counted all nine hundred seconds. Okay, maybe she didn't do a full 'Mississippi' for each second, but it was close enough that the full bladder situation had reached emergency status.

"Kowalski," Jody yelled through her gag, coming out sounding closer to 'kowalpee,' which didn't help take her mind off the business she had to take care of.

After another full counting one hundred and twenty seconds—Mississippis included—there were still no telltale footsteps coming up the stairs.

"Kowalpee!" she screamed louder.

At this point, Jody would take Rodriguez, as long as he let her go to the toilet before her hurt her. If it was him appearing at the doorway, she might not have to worry about the toilet because she was pretty likely to wet the bed in her fear.

Quick footsteps pounded up the stairs and her door swung open revealing, to her relief, Kowalski. Jody pleaded with her eyes for him to understand her plight, but he only stared at her with a puzzled expression. She pressed her knees together and wiggled, not quite sure how to communicate to him without being able to do a potty dance. After a few seconds, understanding dawned and he quickly went to work on removing the ropes.

When Kowalski pulled the ropes away, Jody scrambled off the bed toward the bathroom, only succeeding in falling flat on her face. Crawling desperately toward the door on numb hands and feet, she crossed the threshold just as Kowalski lifted her from the floor and propelled her more than carried her toward the toilet. Jody yanked her pants and underwear down her legs and dropped onto the seat mere seconds before the first drops escaped. The release of pressure on her bladder elicited a drawn out moan from her.

Looking up from her spot on the toilet, Jody was shocked to find Kowalski standing with his back to her. In her panic, she'd almost completely forgotten he was there. At least he'd turned away to give her some modicum of privacy. Not wanting to push her luck, she pulled off a strip of toilet paper, but froze when another set of footsteps sounded on the stairs.

"Finish up," Kowalski hissed over his shoulder, pushing off the doorframe and striding farther into the room.

Kowalski's movement unfroze her brain and Jody quickly wiped and tugged her pants up her legs just as the sound of Rodriguez's voice filled the room.

CHAPTER TEN

*"**Where the fuck** is she?"* Rodriguez demanded.

Jody made it a point to flush the toilet and turn on the sink so Kowalski wouldn't have to answer, but he did anyway. Jody listened to their exchange while frantically untying the cloth holding the gag in her mouth. Maybe they'd forget to put it back on when they tied her back up if she kept quiet.

"She had to take a piss. I didn't want to have to change sheets when she pissed the bed," Kowalski explained to Rodriguez.

"If she pissed the bed, it'd be her own fault. I'd make her lay in it," Rodriguez responded.

"We can already smell more nasty shit than we want to, you really want to add that to the mix?" Kowalski countered, skepticism clear in his voice.

"Fuck no," Rodriguez replied. "Finish the fuck up," he said louder, presumably addressing her.

Jody wiped her hands at a painstakingly slow pace, trying to come up with a plan ... again. She wasn't particularly good with on-the-fly stressful situations and thinking clearly when it wasn't in a hospital setting. There, it was muscle memory. Here, not so much. Alicia had invited her to exactly one of those escape parties where a group of people have to figure out how to get out of a locked room. Her mind went blank when confronted with a crisis situation when it wasn't medically involved, and now was no exception. She had nothing. There was no alternative to stepping foot out her bathroom door and facing the two Vampires who invaded her room and being completely and utterly at their mercy.

Taking small steps, which only delayed the inevitable, Jody moved back into her room. Keeping her eyes trained on the floor, she refused to look up at either of them. She hoped their only plans for her were to tie her back up and put her back in her bed, rather than any one of the other sinister scenarios that began popping in her head.

The moment she cleared the doorway, Rodriguez's large body stood in front of her. Jody let out a gasp. He was so fast, she hardly registered how quickly he got between her an Kowalski. Her eyes met Rodriguez's dark ones and she instantly shrank away. His eyes were like nothing she'd ever seen before. So much violence and nefarious intent emanated from them, and they were focused on her at the moment.

"I missed you," Rodriguez crooned, his smile sending a wave of nausea through Jody. "At least I got to spend some time with your sister while I was away."

Jody glanced down at the blood staining his shirt and her eyes swam with tears. Covering her mouth with her hand, she fought against the sob building in her chest.

"She's quite the fighter, your sister," he chuckled, holding out his shirt to look down at a tear in it surrounded by blood.

The shirt was spattered with blood, but the skin beneath the slice in the fabric was unscathed. Jody had seen enough stab wounds working in the ER, and this certainly looked like one, except the missing hole in his flesh.

"Leave. Now," Kowalski's voice ordered from behind Rodriguez.

The command didn't even faze Rodriguez. Not acknowledging that Kowalski had spoken, he kept his eyes locked on Jody.

"I lost a bit of blood, but I had a snack on the way to take the edge off and heal me up pretty well. One of the nice things about being a Vamp that we didn't have as Hunters." Rodriguez took a step toward her.

Her body's automatic response was to retreat, but her back hit the doorjamb, halting any progress away.

"I could use a little more blood though. Not much, just a few swallows," Rodriguez continued speaking as he advanced.

"She's mine, fuck off," Kowalski growled behind the enormity of Rodriguez.

Rodriguez raised an eyebrow at her. "Yours, huh?" he taunted, his tone mocking both Kowalski and Jody. "Nah, I licked her, she's mine," he said, claiming her like Jody and Alicia used to do when they were kids.

A deep growl sounded from Kowalski, and Jody was terrified she was going to be in the middle of a brawl between two gigantic Vampires. She couldn't see that ending well for her ... or her room, for that matter. Rodriguez whipped around so quickly, it took Jody a second to realize she was now looking at his back instead of his broad chest. A vicious snarl tore from him, but his entire body blocked her view of the rest of the room. The sound of flesh meeting flesh where the two came to blows was her cue to move the hell out of the way.

Edging her way around the doorjamb, Jody backed into the bathroom. The glint of the light off the scissors caught her eye, and she decided now was not a good time to be without a weapon. Scooping the blade up in her hand, she climbed into the tub, brandishing the weapon while she waited to see who would emerge victorious from the brawl. She supposed in some scenarios it might be flattering to have two attractive men fighting over her, but that would be when they were actual men looking for a date or something and not looking to drink her blood. The scissors shook and jumped in her hand with every crash and shout from the Vampires on the other side of the wall.

After another minute, the din settled into silence and Jody waited, her breath coming in desperate gasps. She didn't care who was coming through that doorway, they were getting scissors to the throat. If she had a gun, this would be a shoot to kill kind of scenario, but since there was no firearm to be had, stabbing to kill was the next best thing. Heavy footfalls sounded through the room and made their way to her hiding place. When the shower curtain was pulled away, Jody closed her eyes and swung out and up, estimating where the optimal location would be on the tall Vampires. Her blade never hit their mark though. A meaty fist gripped her wrist and she fought to open her eyes to see who had won.

CHAPTER ELEVEN

"*I was wrong* about you, you might be even more of a firebrand than your sister," Rodriguez's voice pierced into her brain.

Rodriguez. What had he done to Kowalski? Had he killed him? What was he going to do to her? Rodriguez squeezed his grip on her wrist and Jody dropped the scissors with a sob. The clatter of the metal and plastic against the tub echoed loudly in the tiled space. This was it, all lines of defense were gone and she was completely at his mercy.

"Open your eyes. I want you to see how happy it makes me to watch this pretty face twist with pain," Rodriguez commanded, his breath wafting over her, bringing the stench of decaying blood to her nostrils.

Jody had dealt with worse smells in the ER, but knowing the blood clotting in his mouth wasn't his own made it more sickening. She held her breath and squeezed her eyes shut even tighter.

"It won't take much for me to snap it if you don't obey," he warned, applying more pressure to the delicate bones in her wrist.

Taking in a shaky breath, Jody eased her eyes open. A sadistic glee that turned her stomach filled

Rodriguez's gaze. Working in a hospital and helping those injured by others had long ago cemented the knowledge the world wasn't all unicorns and rainbows. There were bad people out there, but Jody wasn't sure she truly believed she'd ever encounter pure evil until she looked upon this Vampire's face.

"Don't worry, I'm not going to kill you. I like coming back for seconds," he reassured before sharp fangs pierced her skin.

Jody let out a pained scream, even knowing she was giving him exactly what he wanted. A low rumble of what she could only describe as pleasure came from Rodriguez as he sucked blood from her. His arm wrapped tight around her like a vise, holding her in place while he took from her. The sharp pain in her neck subsided to a dull ache and instead her attention was focused on the roiling of her stomach with the sensation of ever-increasing pressure accompanying the pull of blood from her vessels.

An eternity passed before she could feel unconsciousness threaten her. He may have said he wasn't going to kill her, but he never said how close he would come. He was definitely close. She'd watched people die from blood loss, powerless to stop it. Now was no exception, but this time she wasn't merely a witness, she was the victim, she knew what it was to experience it.

Rodriguez's mouth unlatched from her skin, and she felt a wave of temporary relief when the pressure was gone. Her body no longer had the energy to command her muscles to keep her neck upright and it lolled to the side. It would be only a matter of time before the loss of blood took its final toll on her body. He'd taken a lot, and the body required rest, food, and water to replenish. She wasn't sure how much, if any of the three she would be getting before he came back for his seconds. Jody felt confident he never went for thirds before moving on to a new meal.

"I couldn't help myself, I had to taste you. Next time, I'll sample the rest of you." He emphasized what exactly it was he intended to sample with a squeeze of her ass cheek.

The turmoil in her stomach returned, and Jody was sure she would have retched all over him if there had been anything in it. She kind of wished there was something to vomit just to see the expression on his face when he was covered in her bile. It would be the only revenge she would get, and now she couldn't even do that. Her eyes drooped heavily and her body sagged against him, his massive arms still wrapped around her like an equally deadly python.

All at once, she found herself lifted into the air and a solid shoulder jammed into her achingly empty stomach. How long had she gone without food? How long had she gone without water? Only a day, she supposed. Had this nightmare only started a day ago?

Jody's limps flopped bonelessly as Rodriguez took graceful steps toward her bed. It was criminal that someone of his size could move with such lithe prowess, but she supposed that was one of those perks of being a lethal, predatory Vampire. Stealth and unmatched grace. It only took half a dozen strides to bring Rodriguez from the edge of the tub in her bathroom to looming over her bed.

With an unceremonious bounce, Rodriguez rolled her off his shoulder and dropped her to the bed. Jody landed with her neck at an odd angle, one she knew would leave her sore if she stayed that way too long, but her muscles weren't listening to her commands to readjust.

"Your sister is running out of time. Tomorrow, sweet thing," Rodriguez threatened, turning from her and walking through the door.

Jody had fully expected her hands and legs to be bound again, however, it wasn't like she could get up and go anywhere when she couldn't even make her neck move so she didn't end up with a crick in it later. She had hoped he would have at least given her some water. He had to know if he took a second meal from her tomorrow, there wasn't going to be much left. No food. No water. At least she was left in peace to engage in the third aspect of the trifecta of blood creation—rest.

Closing her eyes, Jody attempted to drift toward sleep, but trying to relax with her neck at such an odd angle was more than a little uncomfortable. She debated on whether or not losing the last reserves of her energy to get comfortable enough to sleep was worth it ... and decided it was. If it was the last night of sleep she was ever going to get, she wasn't going to do it with her neck half bent beneath her.

An estimated twenty minutes later, Jody managed to straighten out her vertebrae to a position she could live with. Or, rather, sleep in. Sweat beaded her brow with the effort, and her breath came out in pants. She most definitely deserved whatever rest she could coax after those miniscule gymnastics. Giving in to the overwhelming urge to close her eyes, she wondering if it would be the last time she ever did.

CHAPTER TWELVE

"They fucked you up pretty good, didn't they, princess?" a soft voice brought Jody up from the depths of sleep.

She couldn't place the voice. Jody couldn't tell if it was Kowalski or Rodriguez, and right now she was too far gone to be alarmed. They could violate her in a hundred different ways, and she wasn't sure she'd care right now. Okay, she'd care. She was just too exhausted to do a damned thing about it.

"We'll get you good as new soon. Here," the voice came again, and she didn't know what it was she was supposed to be taking, "drink."

A warm liquid she couldn't identify immediately identify hit her lips. She set her mind to work trying. It was more viscous than water, but the taste didn't make sense. It was familiar to her, though. It coated her tongue and slid down the back of her throat, and she fought not to cough as it hydrated the parched tissue there. It was the same taste it in her mouth after Rodriguez's fist connected with her jaw. Blood.

Jody wanted her eyes to fly open in shock, but they slowly eased their way up, making the anticipation of confirming her suspicions as to the origins of what was being poured into her mouth agonizing. When a sliver of the world was visible through cracked eyelids, she supposed it really didn't matter how quickly they opened, because she couldn't see a damned thing anyway. Not only was it dark in her room, but the faint glow of her clock showed her everything was a bit blurry. She could make out a dark figure crouched before her, but it wasn't much more than a silhouette … and not one she recognized, if she could in fact recognize anyone's silhouette.

"Drink it, princess, it'll make you feel better," the silhouette urged.

Jody wasn't going to argue. She wasn't sure she could feel any *worse* unless she was dead, and then she supposed she wouldn't be feeling a damned thing at all. She'd take whatever miracle cure this guy claimed to give her, because if it was something that killed her, maybe she'd be better off. Even in her dazed state, she knew she was in bad shape. Worse than she'd originally thought. She'd never seen anyone recover from as much blood loss as she experienced, especially without any kind of medical assistance.

Bit by bit the edges of the silhouette came into clearer focus. It was definitely male, but she could tell that by his voice. What she didn't know was if he was a *man*. She figured it was highly unlikely given the scenarios from the past several days and the blood now flowing into her mouth. Jody's eyes adjusted to the dim luminescence of her alarm clock in the otherwise pitch black room and she was relieved for a few seconds to see the silhouette belonged to neither Rodriguez nor Kowalski. After those few seconds of initial relief, panic bloomed in her chest—another player had entered the game and he was a complete wild card. She had no idea who he was or whether he was friend or foe. She could reasonably assume friend since he seemed to be helping her, but Kowalski had claimed to want to help her, too. She wasn't going to make the mistake of trusting someone who hadn't earned it a second time.

"There you go," he encouraged, and Jody realized there was still blood flowing into her mouth.

Where was it coming from? She directed her eyes down and saw his wrist was pressed against her mouth. A flurry of concerns involving blood borne pathogens passed through her brain. She'd studied the whole gamut in nursing school, and the reminder of each one of them parading through her brain brought on panic.

"Shh, shh, shh," he crooned, petting her hair for a moment.

Jody tried to pull her head away, thinking of how much fun it would not be to live with HIV or Hepatitis.

"I'm not trying to hurt you, princess," Silhouette reassured, even as his hand gripped her head to keep her from moving. "Just a little more and we can get going."

Going? It was like déjà vu, the scene with Kowalski playing over in her head again. She couldn't leave, not with him. Not with any of them. She didn't know him, and he could be just as deadly as the others, and then no one would find her until she was an empty corpse.

"Hey, it's going to be okay." Pulling his wrist away, he wiped off what she assumed were remnants of his blood from the corners of her mouth with the pads of his fingers. "You're going to be okay. Can you stand?"

Could she stand? What the hell kind of question was that? Hadn't this guy seen what shape she was in when he came in?

"Up you go," he said, pulling her shoulders so she sat up.

Jody waited for the vertigo to hit, along with the nausea, but it was noticeably absent. That was a good sign.

"You ready to stand now?" he encouraged, his face close to hers, but she couldn't make out any of the features. It almost made it easier to put a little bit of faith in a nameless, faceless guy in the dark of her room.

Silhouette swung her feet over the side of the bed for her, then pulled her up with his hands under her arms. Jody felt like a child having to be hoisted into a standing position.

"There you go," he pronounced when she was steadied on her feet.

Slowly, Silhouette removed his hands from her armpits and held them to the side, fingers spread wide open, cautiously waiting for her to topple to the floor. He stood assessing her balance for a moment, before she saw his head move up and down as if making an entirely different assessment of her. Jody tried not to shrink into herself to prevent him from looking. She'd gotten more unwanted attention with similar gazes in the last day or so to last her an entire lifetime.

"You can't go outside like that," he stated, and she was relieved him evaluating her didn't mean there were unsavory intentions on his mind.

Jody glanced down at her pajamas. He was right. Before she could act, he was digging through her closet and dresser, throwing jeans and a hoodie on the bed near her.

"Boots and coat downstairs?" he asked before lifting his gaze from the shoes littering the bottom of her closet.

"Yes," Jody croaked, her voice coming out scratchy and cracked.

"Just put those on over what you're wearing, and we'll get your outside stuff on the way out," he ordered, as if they were just going to walk out her front door without a few Vampires and whatever the hell Micelli was stopping them.

When she didn't move to get dressed, he took a step toward her and she couldn't help taking one away.

"I'm not going to hurt you, princess. You need help getting dressed? We gotta haul ass out of here," he warned, holding his hands up in a show of surrender.

Jody shook her head vigorously. She didn't like the idea of him touching her, even if it was to help her put on clothes. Tentatively, she pulled on the jeans and sweatshirt he laid out for her, lamenting she wouldn't get to take a shower, or put on a bra. When her head popped up through the neck, she watched as Silhouette whipped around and faced the door. His body crouched low, his limbs gone rigid.

"Stay behind me. Better yet, go into the bathroom," he commanded over his shoulder, his attention still glued to the door.

Jody hesitated a few moments before slipping into the bathroom. She didn't like the idea of going back to the scene of Rodriguez's attack, and didn't know how she felt about following the orders of the guy who just appeared in her room. On one hand, he had just done something miraculous with his blood that brought her dying body back to nearly fully functional. On the other, he had done something miraculous with his *blood* that brought her dying body back to nearly fully functional!

Seconds after she pushed the bathroom door almost closed, her bedroom door burst open. A loud growl sounded and she couldn't help peeking through the crack to watch what was about to unfold. Kowalski took on the same crouched stance as Silhouette, looking like a feral animal.

"Who the fuck are you? You can't have her, she's *mine!*" Kowalski snarled out.

Silhouette didn't bother answering before he rushed toward Kowalski. Jody had a hard time keeping up with their movements. Everything was a shadowy blur of flying limbs and landed blows in the dark room. Grunts and growls sounded from the shadows and she couldn't miss the few sickening cracks of breaking bones, along with the howls of pain accompanying them.

Suddenly, a gunshot rang out, the sound temporarily deafening her as it echoed off the walls of her small room. Jody scrambled back from the door and closed it, flipping the lock. She'd been unable to decipher which of them pulled the trigger, but she wasn't waiting to find out. Scrambling on hands and knees toward the window, she shoved it open with her shoulder. The bright moonlight glinted off the snow below and she took a deep breath. She may not have her coat and boots, but at least she had on more than her pajamas. Jody steadied herself before pulling her upper body through the window. After a silent prayer she didn't land on her head or break any vital limbs, she shoved against the exterior wall of the house.

A hand snaked around her ankle and she let out a scream and tried to kick him off, not caring which *him* it was at this point. Another hand wrapped around her other ankle and she felt herself being dragged back into captivity.

"You're going to break your fucking legs if you jump from there!" Silhouette chided as he yanked on her, effectively dislodging the grip she had on the outside of the house.

His hands gripped her body roughly as he managed to pull her all the way inside.

"Let me go!" she screamed, kicking and hitting anything she could.

A scream of pain burst from her when her fist met solid drywall.

"Oh for fuck's sake," Silhouette swore, wrapping his arms around her to keep her from flailing. "I can't give you any more blood right now."

Jody had no idea what that meant. Well, she thought she might have an idea of what that meant, because when she'd first come in the bathroom, she caught a little glimpse of herself in the mirror, and although she looked more than a little bedraggled, her face was no longer bruised and busted up. Miraculous healing blood. Pure insanity.

The throbbing in her hand began pulling all Jody's attention away from Silhouette hoisting her body up and carrying her from the bathroom. She cradled it against her chest, just knowing she broke *something*.

"Time to go, princess," he proclaimed, stepping through her room.

Jody peered down at Kowalski's body lying still on her floor, his blood seeping out into a great pool soaking into her carpet.

"You killed him?" she couldn't help but ask. She didn't know if Vampires could die the same way as humans, but she could imagine a gunshot in the right place might do the trick.

"Yeah," Silhouette answered dispassionately while carting her down the stairs.

A shudder ran through her at the callous way he dismissed taking a life, even a Vampire one. Jody was getting all kinds of acquainted with killers lately, and she was none too happy about it. She preferred her villains to keep to the screens and pages where she could safely tuck them away when they got to be too much.

Silhouette set her on her feet when they reached the bottom of the stairs and then tossed her coat at her.

"Put it on," he ordered, looking around. "Where are your boots?"

"They're by the back door." Jody gingerly pulled her broken hand through the sleeve.

Silhouette was gone all of two seconds before reappearing with her boots. Well, she was definitely getting the vibe he firmly belonged in the Vampire category. Crouching down at her feet, he guided each one into the boots with hurried motions. When his head whipped up and stared at the door, Jody instantly knew something was wrong.

"They were supposed to be hunting. Fuck, fuck, fuck," he chanted under his breath.

The front door burst open and Rodriguez's large body came lumbering through it. Silhouette pulled out a gun and fired a shot, clipping Rodriguez in the shoulder when he dodged out of the way. Jody stood frozen in terror at the sight of Rodriguez again. A hard shove from Silhouette pushed her to the ground, thawing her brain enough to scramble out of the way when the two Vampire's bodies clashed together.

Silhouette let out a howl of pain when Rodriguez wrenched on his arm, and Jody could see in the dim light he'd dislocated it. Her stomach surged at the sights and sounds, threatening to bring the blood Silhouette fed her back up. Closing her eyes and covering her ears, Jody concentrated on breathing and keeping her stomach intact.

Another gunshot rang out and Jody's eyes flew open when Rodriguez's body landed with a thud not two feet from where she cowered. She let out a surprised screech and scrambled farther away.

"Let's go!" Silhouette shouted, scooping her up with his undamaged arm and charging through the door.

CHAPTER THIRTEEN

The cool air hit Jody in the face and she pulled in a surprised gasp. She was thankful they'd had time and her rescuer had the foresight to get her in some winter appropriate clothing. Her entire body jostled with each step Silhouette took and she cradled her broken hand closer to her chest to keep it from bumping into anything and causing more of those super wonderful shooting pains which stole her breath away.

Opening the passenger door of a truck idling just down the street from her house, Silhouette slid Jody into the seat and snapped the buckle in place, then slipped into the driver's side. The door barely clicked shut before the truck lurched forward and they were speeding down the road.

The tension in the truck was palpable and Jody watched Silhouette glance up from the road to the rearview mirror every few seconds. When they made it a few miles from her house, he glanced at her instead. Jody shrunk back when his eyes landed on her, huddling against the door.

"Do you really think I'd hurt you after all that?" he chided, irritation evident in his tone.

Jody flinched at his tone, but didn't avert her eyes. She attempted to study him in the muted glow of light provided by the truck's dash, but could make out even less of him than what she saw in her room.

"Who are you?" she whispered, realizing she couldn't call him 'Silhouette' for the duration of the time they would be spending together ... hopefully that duration would be very short.

"Zeke," he announced, holding out his hand across his body for her to shake.

All right, she had a name now, but she still didn't know why she was in his truck.

Jody stared down at his hand like it would bite her if she got any closer. He looked down at it, too, and after realizing she wasn't going to voluntarily touch him, placed it back on the steering wheel.

"What about you, princess, you got a name?" he asked, glancing over at her quickly before returning his attention to the road.

What the hell? He'd broken into her house and killed at least one Vampire in the process of pulling her out of a pretty horrific scenario and he didn't even know who she was?

"How did you know to come rescue me?" she questioned.

"Jackson called me, asked me to get you out," he confessed with a shrug, like it was no big deal what he'd just done, and like she should know who the hell Jackson was.

"Who's Jackson?" Jody demanded. She knew he wasn't intentionally being cryptic, but only getting these tiny pieces of information at a time was really taking its toll.

"Hey now, if you want me to answer questions, you have to answer some, too," he chastised with playful smile.

How can he be smiling like that after what just happened? Never mind that his shoulder is dislocated, isn't he in pain? She sure as hell was. Jody watched him for a moment as he steered with one hand easily, the other laying in his lap.

"Stop the truck," she demanded. She supposed the least she could do was help him get his shoulder back in place after what he'd done for her.

"Excuse me?" Zeke said with a chuckle that annoyed her, like she was off her rocker.

"Let me help you with your shoulder," Jody offered, pointing to where his hand lay limply in his lap. "I'm a nurse."

Zeke released a hearty laugh, though she couldn't see what was so damned funny. "I'm not stopping the truck until we've put another ten miles between us and them," he explained, and she couldn't miss how he'd put them in the same category. Us versus them.

Jody tried to cross her arms to take on a more intimidating posture, but winced when she bumped her hand. Stubborn men.

"Tell you what. When we get far enough out, I'll stop. You can help me with my shoulder and I'll help you with your hand. Deal?" he offered, glancing over at her.

The appeal of getting a bit more of that miracle blood to heal her hand more than overshadowed Jody's need to let the nurse within take charge and order him to allow her help immediately. She nodded silently and turned to face out the window. It was still dark outside, but she could see the illumination of the waning moon through the thin veil of clouds. Not knowing much about the phases of the moon or its location in the sky and what that meant, Jody had no idea what time it was just by looking at it. She went with the more modern version of telling time and glanced at the clock on the dash. It was a few minutes shy of four thirty in the morning. On a normal day, she would be waking up to the blaring of her alarm clock in another hour.

"Are you going to tell me your name, or am I just going to keep calling you princess?" Zeke asked, breaking into the silence.

"It's Jody. Now can you tell me who Jackson is now and why he sent you to come get me?"

A perplexed expression crossed Zeke's face. "Jackson asked me to come get you as a favor to his girl. You're her sister, right?"

His girl? Alicia?

"Are you talking about Alicia?" Jody puzzled.

"Fuck, I didn't get her name either. He just asked me and I said I would," Zeke admitted, shaking his head.

"What do you get out of this? Helping me, I mean," Jody pressed, skipping over the real question she wanted to ask, though she was pretty sure she knew the answer.

"Are you asking me if I'm getting paid to help you?" he scoffed, and Jody was pretty sure he sounded offended. "He helped me once, so I'm returning the favor."

The question surged forth from her mouth before she could stop from blurting it out, "Are you a Vampire?"

"I think we're done with questions. Let's just get you back to your sister," he bit out, effectively shutting down her question.

"I didn't mean to offend—" Jody started, but Zeke didn't let her finish.

"I'm not offended by your question, I'm offended that you still think I'm going to hurt you after I pulled your ass out of hell," he huffed and shook his head.

Zeke maneuvered the truck to the side of a little service station which appeared to be the only thing open in the sleepy hours of the morning. Slamming the truck into park, Jody flinched at the force behind it.

"I think you'll excuse me if I'm not exactly trusting of strangers right now," she retorted when he turned to look at her. She reached for the door handle to let herself out.

"Oh no you don't," he said with a chuckle as he gripped her wrist. "You can't go out there."

Cold terror washed over her. It was just like she'd imagined. She'd moved from one instance of captivity to another.

"Fucking-a, princess! I know you're a little shook up and all, but you need to get a grip," Zeke admonished, still holding her wrist tightly. At least it was her uninjured one.

Jody's anger flared. Telling her to get a grip after everything she'd been through was the equivalent of telling a woman to calm down.

"Get a grip?" she shouted, edging her face closer to his. "Are you fucking serious right now? Do you have any idea what I've been through the last twenty-four hours?"

"No, I don't. But I've got a pretty good idea based on the state I found you in," he confessed with a smirk.

"You think this is fucking funny?" Jody screamed at him.

"No, ma'am, but this is sure a hell of a lot better than having you cower every time I look in your direction." He was trying to rile her up on purpose.

"You're an asshole," she told him, but the words had no bite in them. The flames he'd stirred up died back down to embers.

"So I've been told," Zeke said with a chuckle. "You can't go out there because a, there's no one here, so there's nowhere to go. And two, you're covered in blood."

Jody glanced down, and sure enough she could see the dark smears of blood on her neck through the collar of her sweatshirt. She bet it was all in her hair, too. "You can't count a and then go to two," she mumbled petulantly.

"I do believe I just did." Zeke smirked, releasing his hold on her hand, seeming to be satisfied she saw his logic in not leaving the truck. "Do you mind?" He nodded down to his injured arm.

"You first," Jody demanded, nodding down to her hand. "I can't exactly put a shoulder back in place with one hand."

Jody could see the dim light reflect off the bright whites of his teeth when he gave her a big smile.

"Fair enough," he agreed, and brought the wrist of his other hand to his mouth and bit down.

Jody didn't realize there was a very distinguishable sound that accompanied teeth tearing through flesh. She did now and hoped it wouldn't be one she'd be hearing again anytime soon.

"You going to be all right over there?" Zeke worried. "You look a little green."

"How can I look green? Everything in here looks black," she retorted, turning her face from him and pressing it against the cool glass of the window.

"I can see you just fine," he stated, and she could almost imagine it accompanied a wink. She would never know for sure, though, because she couldn't pull her suddenly feverish forehead from the blessed cold of the glass. "Take deep breaths, because if you barf up my blood, I'm not giving you more."

Jody nodded, not having the concentration to focus on not vomiting *and* coming up with a snarky retort. When she no longer felt as though she was going to pass out or throw up, she turned back to where Zeke waited and watched her patiently.

"I'm ready," she proclaimed, taking in a deep breath and steeling herself for whatever came next. She imagined it might be a little more difficult to ingest blood when she was so much more alert and aware of what was filling her mouth.

"Come on over," he encouraged, gesturing to a spot next to him on the bench seat.

Jody inched over warily, now more worried about jostling her hand than what Zeke might do to her. When she got within a few inches, he held out his wrist where blood welled from some nasty looking bites.

"Let's get a move on before they close up. I don't think you'll make it if I have to open up new ones," Zeke encouraged with a sigh.

"Ass," she mumbled before she brought his wrist to her mouth.

Jody fought her gag reflex when she first licked at the blood welling from the lacerations and swallowed them from her tongue. She didn't know how much she would need.

"Suck," he urged, and she couldn't help the blush that crept up her cheeks at the way her mind went to the gutter when he gave the single word order. Jody was glad he couldn't see the tinge of her skin in the darkness. "Dirty girl," he chuckled, and her blush deepened.

Jody widened her lips around the wound and created suction, pulling blood from the wound and swallowing it down. Each tiny mouthful took enormous effort and she was grateful her first experience with his blood had been in a nearly unconscious state. She imagined he'd sacrificed a lot of his blood to her to heal the kind of wounds she'd had.

"That ought to do it," Zeke announced, his voice sounding strained.

Jody pulled her lips off him with a wet smack and forced herself to swallow down the last of what remained in her mouth. Wiping the back of her hand across her lips, she didn't realize until she was finished it was with her previously injured hand.

"Amazing," she whispered, examining her hand. Flexing her fingers one by one, she wiggled them all in turn until Zeke clearing his throat pulled her back.

"You mind?" he asked, eyebrows raised.

A look of apprehension crossed his face and was gone quickly. Jody wondered if he was worried *she* was going to hurt *him* or if he was worried she wasn't going to help him at all. She debated it for a second. Although he'd been an ass, he still made good on his end of the deal.

After positioning her hands in the right places on his arm and shoulder, Jody stared up at him.

"You ready?" she asked, and he nodded. "Okay, on the count of three—"

"Don't fucking count, just do it," he growled, clearly in pain from where she gripped him.

"One," Jody started her countdown anyway; it was almost like she couldn't do it without the count. "Two!" she announced and pulled.

"Fuck," Zeke hissed between clenched teeth. "I knew you were going to do that."

Jody couldn't help but chuckle. Zeke rolled his shoulder around a little bit and flexed it.

"Doesn't your blood heal you, too? How come that didn't just, you know, pop back into place on its own?" she questioned, not really knowing if that's how it would work.

"It would have eventually, after I fed. It's slower when I've lost a fair amount of blood," he explained, lifting his rear off the seat and patting at his pockets.

"Oh," Jody acknowledged. He'd put himself at risk in more ways than one to get her out of that house.

"Don't worry, I'm not going to ask you to be my next meal, princess," he said with a chuckle, now sticking his hands in his coat pockets and patting each of them in turn. When he turned to her, she could barely make out the contours of his face, but the anguish in his voice was evident. "My phone's gone."

CHAPTER FOURTEEN

Zeke's announcement didn't register the same near-panic in her as it clearly did in him.

"Okay."

"If I don't have my phone, I can't call Jackson to let him know I've got you safe and sound," Zeke told her, stuffing his hand between the creases in the seat.

"I know it's not really polite to show up on someone's doorstep unannounced, but I think they'd make an exception if we just went to where they are."

"I don't know where they are," he explained, still in the throes of his frantic search.

"I'm not following," Jody admitted, rubbing her fingers into her eyes. It had been a long day and she really just wanted to find Alicia and crash wherever she was.

"I don't have the location of the lab. We kept it that way so if my retrieval was unsuccessful, Micelli's guys couldn't see the location in my blood. Although, if you want my opinion, that fucker already knows a hell of a lot more than what your friends think he knows, and that includes the location of their *secret* lab," Zeke explained, making air quotes with his fingers when referencing the secret lab.

"So, I hear you talking but there are a few phrases in there just not really ringing any bells." Jody shook her head, feeling increasingly in need of some sleep.

"You really don't know anything about what's going on, do you?" Zeke questioned, halting his frantic search to face her. Even though she couldn't see much of him in the dark, he was obviously surprised.

"Nope. A little bit of home invasion the night before last and a whole lot of terror. I did learn Vampires exist, though, so that was fun," she divulged, running her hand along her neck where Rodriguez bit her.

"Hmm." Zeke rubbed his hand across his chin, the sound of his stubble against callused hands too loud in the quiet. "Well, you'll learn about blood memories soon enough. And as soon as we figure out a way to get ahold of Jackson, you'll get to learn all about their science experiment which is the worst kept secret in the Vampire world."

"Riddles," Jody sighed to herself. She was much too tired for these kinds of games.

"You'll see. I wouldn't want to spoil your surprises." She could see the dim light gleaming off his teeth again as he smiled. "In the meantime," he announced loudly, settling back into his seat, "we both need a little shut eye."

"I can't deny I'm freaking exhausted," she confessed, slumping back into her seat.

"Then it's decided." He put the truck into gear.

~ 90 ~

"What's decided?" Jody asked, her head rolling lazily along the seat to look in his general direction.

"We're going to my place," Zeke answered, turning to watch behind them as he backed the truck out of the parking space.

"I don't remember deciding that." A frown drew down her eyebrows; Jody wasn't too keen on the idea of going home with a Vampire. "What about finding my sister?"

"There's nothing I can do right now short of driving around the city aimlessly. Neither of us have a way to get in touch with them, so there's no point in worrying about it until we figure something out. You're safe, so we might as well both get some rest."

Pulling the truck out onto the road, Zeke wound through sleepy neighborhoods. Jody watched the houses pass by and felt her eyelids droop at the hypnotic sight.

"She's going to be worried," Jody mumbled. If Alicia knew this Jackson guy was sending Zeke for her, and they didn't hear back, she was going to be concerned.

"Yep," he admitted, letting the 'p' come out with a pop. "I promise it will be easier to figure out once we've both had some rest."

Jody was in no position to argue. She could barely keep her eyes open and every thought she'd ever had was jumbled together in her brain. For a few more minutes, she watched Zeke navigate down a maze of roads. There was no way she would ever remember how they'd gotten here or how to get back, so she didn't even try. The truck slowed and Zeke turned into the alley behind a small house just like the one her grandma had lived before she passed away. The place was tiny, probably no bigger than Alicia's condo. Turning off the truck, Zeke turned to her.

"This is where you live?" Jody questioned skeptically.

"Yep. What did you expect? A cave? Maybe some kind of crypt?" Zeke laughed.

"I guess I had no idea *what* to expect, but I didn't expect it to be so close to other people or to look like my grandma's house." She reached for the door.

"Your grandma has good taste," he chuckled. Jody didn't bother to correct his 'has' to 'had.'

When Jody pushed her door open, she hoped she would at least catch a glimpse of Zeke when the light came on, but none did. Feeling slightly disappointed, she slid from the truck and startled backward, slamming her head against the open door when Zeke stood in front of her.

"Do me a favor and don't try to run, okay," he advised while eying her warily. "You may not care much for me, but there are worse alternatives out there, believe you me."

She did believe him. She'd encountered several of them.

"I'm not planning on going anywhere except to bed," Jody told him, her exhaustion coming through loud and clear.

"Come on then, let's find you one," he offered with one of those signature dude nods toward the house.

He turned on his heel, and Jody followed his lead up to the stoop. Pausing for a moment, he pulled keys from his pocket. It seemed too mundane, a Vampire having to lock their door. Jody watched with tired fascination at something so commonplace while she rubbed her hands together to keep warm. It was freaking cold out. Without her phone, she had no idea just *how cold,* but it was definitely in the range of what she and her sister affectionately referred to as 'booger freezing' temperatures. She glanced back at the truck parked under the open sky and kind of felt bad for anyone without an attached garage.

"You coming?" Zeke prodded from the open doorway.

Nodding, Jody hurried inside.

"I'll save the tour for later," he assured, toeing off his boots and hanging his coat on a hook next to the door. It was all so domestic and seemed at odds with her idea of Vampires.

Jody followed suit and pulled off her boots and coat, putting them in their proper places. Once she was done, Zeke turned without a word and headed down a darkened hallway. Jody peered after him, but could barely make out even his silhouette in the pre-dawn darkness.

"Can I, um, turn on a light?" she asked, taking a tentative step into the pitch black where anyone or any*thing* could be waiting for her.

"Here, I'll lead you," Zeke offered, grabbing her hand and eliciting a gasp. She'd expected his hand to be cold from the air outside, but it was warm and comforting wrapped around hers.

"This is a pretty crazy trust exercise," Jody joked shakily while he tugged her forward.

As they stepped down the hallway, Jody flailed her other hand to the side to make sure she didn't run into anything he knew better to dodge. Her feet transitioned from slippery hardwood to plush carpet and she couldn't help but let out a sigh of relief. A little click sounded in the darkness and a soft glow burst forth from a small bedside lamp. The sudden intrusion of light temporarily blinded her. When she opened her eyes, Zeke was standing so close, she took a reflexive step back.

In the light she could finally see what he looked like. Her eyes took him in from head to toe and she started to wonder where they made these Vampires because holy fucking shit he was hot. She had been able to tell from his silhouette that he was a big guy, tall and broad, but she thought some of that might have been the puff from his jacket. She was seeing, however, that was not the case—there was a whole lot of muscle hidden under the long-sleeved tee he donned. Her eyes traveled up to the angular jaw covered in what she estimated was a day or so growth, up to a slightly crooked nose. She could imagine with the way he'd fought tonight it had been broken several times over. When her eyes finally met his she gasped and took another step back.

His pupils were contracted to pinpoints and his eyes nearly glowed a chocolate brown color. The intent way he was staring at her made her shiver, in a surprisingly good way.

"Get a good look?" he teased, cocking his head to the side.

Jody's cheeks burned red as she nodded. She turned her attention to survey the room, hoping Zeke would go about his business and leave her to crawl between the covers of the inviting bed she stood next to. But he didn't move. When she brought her eyes back to him, she saw his gaze was locked on her neck. Her pulse. There was no mistaking the hunger in his eyes. She imagined he might expect to be paid for his rescue with the only currency she had. Blood.

"Are you going to bite me?" Jody whispered, her voice wobbling with fear.

"No, princess. I'm not going to bite you," Zeke sighed, closing his eyes and breathing out deeply. "You can sleep here, I'll be back in a little while." He headed toward the door.

Panic lanced through Jody.

"You're leaving me here alone?" Jody rushed toward him, not realizing she'd clutched onto his sleeve until he peered down at her hand. She promptly dropped it and took a step back, trying to control her heartbeat.

"I have to go… out," he insisted, avoiding her eyes. "You'll be safe here."

"Are you going to kill someone?" she whispered, covering her mouth with a hand in horror.

"No," he stressed defensively, scowling at her. "I'll be back soon. Try to get some sleep. There are clean towels in the cupboard in the bathroom if you want to shower. You can borrow whatever you find in the dresser to sleep in," he recited, waving to the dresser across the room.

Jody turned to look at where Zeke gestured, and when she turned back to plead with him not to leave her here unprotected, he was gone. The roar of the truck outside told her she was too late.

CHAPTER FIFTEEN

Staring at the bed longingly, Jody's thoughts drifted to the shower Zeke had mentioned. Pulling at the loose strands of her hair, she cringed when they crinkled beneath her fingers. There was no way she was going to crawl into bed like this.

After a steaming shower, and rifling through Zeke's dresser for a T-shirt and gym shorts, Jody crawled between the cool sheets. She didn't actually remember lying down before she floated away to sleep.

She ran down a wide open expanse of grass, a feeling of elation bolstering her to pump her legs faster. A shout from her right drew her attention. A glance over her shoulder revealed a boy running at her heels, gaining on her. This kid had to be freaking Olympic runner material to keep up with her.

Out of nowhere, something ran into her, taking her to the ground. No way was it the kid, he was tiny! He definitely didn't look strong enough to tackle her when she got that first glance of him. When her body hit the ground, the impact pushed the air right out of her. Once she was finally able to pull in some oxygen, the throbbing pain in her left shin drew her attention.

A few moments passed before Jody realized she had been rolled onto her back and childlike wailing reached her ears. The sound was so close, she hoped it was from the kid who tackled her—served him right, the little shit. Jody tried to open her eyes and found they weren't responding to her commands. Why wouldn't they open? She wanted to see how badly her leg was hurt. Did she need a hospital, or just some first aid?

"Rob!" a far off voice yelled, but Jody heard loud footsteps pounding closer. "No tackling, Rob. That's what touch means, no tackling!"

The voice had gotten closer with the footsteps, and Jody wanted desperately for the crying to stop so she could hear herself enough to think and tell the man coming toward her she wasn't playing football and this kid just attacked her out of nowhere.

"Let's take a look," the man's voice sounded, but Jody still couldn't force her eyes to open.

Was she unconscious? In a coma? Dear God, she hoped she wasn't in a coma.

"A little bit of blood, but nothing's broken. Open your eyes, Ezekiel, and take a look," the man encouraged, a heavy hand landing on her shoulder.

Jody's eyes opened ... finally. Then she looked down at a skinned up knee and shin. It was covered in blood. When she saw it, she quickly assessed she would need to clean it out and bandage it up as soon as she found a first aid kit. The wailing got louder and Jody's vision was blurred with tears. She wanted to raise her hands to cover her ears, but her arms protested the command.

"We'll get you bandaged up, good as new, son," the man assured her.

Jody turned her head and caught sight of a handsome middle-aged man. His eyes were a familiar chocolate brown.

"Blood scares me," the child wailed. He was so close, but where was he?

A glance around revealed *she* was the crying child.

"Wake up, princess," a deep voice rumbled in her ear. "You're safe."

Jody held her hand over her pounding head, wondering what she'd done last night and who the guy next to her was. She must have had *a lot* to drink if she couldn't remember bringing a guy home. Or going home with him. Cracking an eye open, she was startled out of sleepiness by the face lying inches from hers. It all came back to her in a rush, and so did the weird dreams she had last night. The last one the most vivid.

"I don't want to know which one you saw," Zeke remarked with a grin.

"Which what?" Jody puzzled, covering her mouth with her hand so she didn't breathe morning breath on him.

"Blood memory," he replied.

"Wait, that was *you* in my dream? *I* was *you*? Oh my God," she gasped.

"Yep, but it wasn't a dream. Your blood carries memories of when your blood has been spilled or you've spilled the blood of another," he recited in a bored tone.

"So, you—" Jody started, but Zeke's finger on her lips quieted her.

"I've already lived through each of those experiences, I don't want to live through them again," he said, and Jody could see pain behind his eyes. "Now, are you hungry?"

"Yes," Jody acknowledged warily.

Giving a short nod, Zeke climbed from the bed. Jody watched him walk toward the open closet and literally wiped at her chin to make sure she wasn't drooling. Holy hotness. He stood in a pair of boxer briefs while sifting through the shirts before pulling a cream long-sleeved Henley out and put it on, covering up a full back tattoo before she could make out what it was. Jody wasn't sure the fabric was going to contain so much muscle. She had always been a sucker for muscles and tattoos, and Zeke certainly wasn't lacking either. Her eyes watched his tight ass flex while he pulled on a pair of pajama pants emblazoned with snowflakes. She almost giggled but stopped herself.

"Was it a good show?" Zeke inquired when he turned and slid his feet into slippers.

Busted. His deep brown eyes caught hers and a knowing smirk tugged at the corners of his mouth. Jody tried to hide her bright red face in the covers, but knew he'd already seen it. When she heard his footsteps retreat from the room, she finally lifted her head to make sure he was gone before burying her head in the pillow and letting out a groan. Why did the hottest guy she'd ever seen have to be a Vampire?

After wallowing in her mortification for getting caught ogling him, Jody threw back the covers with determination. She wasn't going to miss breakfast just because the man … Vampire caught her checking him out. He clearly knew he was hot and that she'd look. There was no shame in that, right? She padded over to the closet and surveyed his clothing, eying up a University of Minnesota hoodie that looked like she might drown in, but might not ever get cold in despite the negative temperatures outside. Dropping the shirt over her head, Jody giggled at how it fit more like a dress than a shirt on her. The scent of pine and the outdoors enveloped her, and she had to stifle the urge to press the fabric to her nose and fill her lungs with it. It was heaven.

Jody debated on whether she should put her jeans back on, but couldn't stomach the thought of wearing them again until they were washed. Even though she only wore them for a short time, she imagined there was blood on them somewhere, and that imagined blood was enough to convince her to find alternative means of covering her legs. If she had been more of a temptress, she would have traipsed out into the kitchen with only his hoodie on, but she was far too practical for that. It was like negative ten degrees outside, and she wouldn't be sacrificing warmth for trying to look sexy. At least this morning.

She mentally slapped herself for even thinking about trying to look sexy for him. There were all kinds of things wrong with that train of thought. First and foremost, he was a dangerous Vampire. He *killed* people ... or at least other Vampires. Jody hadn't seen him kill anyone else, but she had to imagine it was an occupational hazard of being what he was. Secondly, she was never the type of woman to attract the devastatingly handsome men. They usually stuck to their own kind—too gorgeous to touch. That wasn't her, and she knew it, and she was okay with it. All the more reason to put any thoughts of him in just his underwear out of her head. Which of course made her think about him in his underwear again. This time she *actually* slapped herself, instead of just mentally.

The aroma of cooking bacon caught her nose and she let it lead her toward the kitchen. On her way down the short hallway, Jody peeked into the open doorways. She'd already seen the bathroom last night on one side of the hallway, and across from it was what appeared to be a gym. The end of the hallway opened into a living room area that flowed into the kitchen. Jody stopped when she reached the living room, searching for signs of a rumpled couch or some stray blanket to indicate he'd slept out here and not next to her in his bed. But there was nothing pointing to that conclusion.

With her nose literally stuck in the air, Jody walked into the kitchen and nearly swooned at the sight of Zeke at the stove, flipping bacon and eggs.

"How do you like your eggs?" he questioned, looking up at her with a smile.

Wow, I could get used to that. And that was as dangerous a thought as they come.

"Um, over medium," she answered, sliding onto a stool at the counter facing his back.

How was she going to keep her tongue in her head around him? Jody watched every bunch and flex of his shoulder muscles through that shirt as he flipped her egg with just a toss of the pan. The sight was just as mouthwatering as the scent of bacon wafting through the air.

"That shirt looks good on you," Zeke complimented, turning to face her with a wink.

Jody glanced down at the shirt engulfing her whole body.

"It looked comfy," Jody admitted with a shrug.

She'd kept the hood up in an attempt to not only ward off the cold, but to hide her awesome bedhead. She could only imagine how much thrashing she'd done in her sleep to earn the tangles she would be spending more than a few minutes trying to comb out later.

"Orange juice?" he offered, taking a glass down from the cupboard and pausing, waiting for her answer.

"That would be great," she replied, her mouth watering at the thought of the cool liquid.

Zeke set the glass in front of her and she drank it down in one breath.

"Mmmm," Jody moaned when she swallowed the last mouthful.

When she opened her eyes—she hadn't even realized she'd closed them—to set the glass down, Zeke was staring at her.

"I'm sorry, I was really thirsty, I guess," she apologized with a little laugh, looking down at her now-empty glass.

"I guess so," he chuckled, removing the carton from the fridge and pouring her another.

After replacing the carton, he pulled out a plate and slid eggs and bacon onto it before setting it in front of her, complete with a fork.

"Oh my God, that smells heavenly. Thank you," she commented, digging in.

Jody was halfway through with her egg and her bacon was completely gone before she realized his eyes were still on her. She had to wonder what it must be like for him to watch people eat now that he didn't anymore. Or did he? She knew woefully little about real Vampires.

"Can I ask you something?" Jody queried, moving a bit of egg white around her plate with her fork.

"Green," he answered, and she looked up at him with surprise.

"What?" she laughed.

"That's my favorite color. That's what you were going to ask me, wasn't it?" he guessed, and she could see laughter dancing in his eyes, even though the rest of his face stayed an emotionless mask.

"Nope, I was actually going to ask what your second favorite was," she retorted with a smirk.

"Oh, that's easy, it's blue." Shrugging, he sipped from a mug she hadn't realized he held in his hands.

"Oh my God, please tell me that's coffee?" she demanded, staring longingly at the mug.

Letting out a hearty laugh, Zeke pulled a mug down from the cupboard and filled it with the nectar of the gods before handing it over to her.

"So, you can, uh, have things other than, um, blood?" she stammered, keeping her eyes trained on the coffee as she brought it to her lips.

"A little here and there," he avoided with a shrug. "I could never quite kick the coffee habit."

"I live on the stuff," she confessed with a laugh. "Especially night shifts at the hospital."

"So what did you really want to ask?" Zeke questioned, his face turning serious.

"Did you sleep in the same bed with me?" she asked cautiously.

It seemed like such a stupid thing to worry about with everything else going on around her, she felt like an idiot the instant the words left her mouth.

"Yes. I started on the couch, but you were crying in your sleep. I didn't know if you were having nightmares or seeing a blood memory. I couldn't get you to wake up, so I just, uh, held you and you stopped crying," he admitted with an uncomfortable laugh and rubbed his hand along the back of his neck.

"You held me?" Jody questioned slowly, trying to process that not only had he slept in the same bed as her all night, but he was *touching* her the whole time.

"Yeah," Zeke sighed and took a sip of his coffee.

CHAPTER SIXTEEN

Jody and Zeke stared at each other in silence for a few minutes, and the longer they did the more Jody felt completely mortified. He'd seen her at her worst and had to hold her in her sleep because she was a complete basket case.

"I'm so sorry," she groaned, lowering her head into her hands.

"Hey, it's not a big deal. It made you feel better, so I was happy to help. I mean, come on, you *are* a lot prettier when you're not covered in blood."

She couldn't hold in the laugh bursting from her at the comic relief.

"I mean, I'm just really sorry to disrupt your life like this. I'm sure you're usually sleeping now or something and I'm keeping you awake and invading your home and wearing your clothes," Jody rambled, picking at the mammoth sweatshirt she was wearing.

"Princess, we're going back to bed as soon as you're finished eating," Zeke ordered, nodding down to the last remaining bite of egg lying speared on her fork. "You need a lot more rest. We both do."

The way he said "we" sent warmth flowing through her and Jody had to stop herself from taking her thoughts in the wrong direction. He didn't mean what her dirty mind wanted him to mean. They were going to *sleep* and nothing more.

After she popped the last piece of egg in her mouth, Zeke took her plate to the sink where he washed it and her fork, placing everything in the drying rack. Jody supposed he didn't have to do much for dishes, seeing as he didn't really eat a whole lot outside his diet of blood. But it made her wonder why, then, he had food and seemingly a fully equipped kitchen. All thoughts of asking him that line of questioning evaporated when he held out his arm, gesturing to the exit.

"Shall we?" he asked.

Jody bit her lip as she passed by him. Was he going to sleep on the couch again? Or was he going to follow her to the bedroom? When Zeke didn't take a detour to the couch and continued to follow her down the hallway, her heart started to race and her palms grew slick with sweat. At the threshold, her movements became robotic as she made her way to the same side of the bed she'd slept on earlier. She dropped the oversized sweatshirt to the floor and the pants she'd borrowed quickly joined them.

"Jody," Zeke said, and her head snapped up to meet his gaze, "It's just sleeping. I'm not going to hurt you." His eyes filled with concern and she believed every word he said.

She did notice he made no such promises about not touching her, and she was actually thankful. If she had another bad dream, she felt better knowing he would be there to comfort her.

"Okay," she managed to croak out and slid into bed.

A small sigh escaped Jody when the squishy mattress pad cradled her body. She listened as Zeke slid into his side and she was painfully aware of how close he really was. The bed was a queen or a full, she couldn't really tell, but he was a big guy and took up his entire half. That left only about a foot of space between them. Once he made himself comfortable and the sounds of shifting bedding subsided, the room was painfully quiet, highlighting the awkwardness she felt.

"'Night, princess," Zeke said quietly.

Jody couldn't help smiling. "'Night."

Somehow just that little exchange was all she needed to calm her entire being down enough to drift off to sleep.

"Hey!" Jody shouted, but it came out in Zeke's voice.

Here we go again.

Stepping outside what seemed to be a bar, Jody was clothed in Zeke's body. Her gaze was trained on the man and a woman Zeke was shouting at. Jody's stomach sank when she realized the man had a hand around the woman's throat, holding her in place, while his other slapped her across the face. The woman clawed at her assailant's fingers, her legs kicking wildly trying to make contact.

"What the hell do you think you're doing?" Zeke yelled, running toward them.

"How about you mind your own fucking business, huh?" the man snarled, when Zeke got close enough to hear.

The man stopped his assault enough to take notice of Zeke continuing his approach, but didn't run like Jody expected he might.

Instead, the asshole turned without bothering to remove his hand from the woman's throat. A sneer graced the man's face as Zeke got closer. He shoved the woman to the ground and crouched low.

"Help!" the woman screamed, backing away on hands and knees from where Zeke and the attacker stood still in a standoff.

"Call the cops," Zeke ordered her in a calm voice, but Jody could feel the nervous energy rolling off him.

The guy in front of him was huge and aggressive. Jody was sure Zeke could hold his own against a guy like this if they were maybe sparring in a ring or something where the moves were more calculation than emotion, but with the way his opponent was looking at him, all bets were not in Zeke's favor.

At the mention of the police, the man made the first move and swung at Zeke. His gaze was still on the woman, and he just barely blocked the jab to his gut. The asshole followed up with a right hook Zeke wasn't fast enough to dodge, and then a kick to the abdomen he missed with his first swing. Zeke doubled over, trying to catch his breath, and Jody screamed at him in her head to look up … but by the time he did, it was too late.

The unmistakable sound of the metallic click of a knife opening drew Jody's attention. It was a sound ingrained in her memory from when her father would take out his Swiss Army knife on camping trips to cut branches for roasting marshmallows around the campfire. When Zeke did finally look up, it was too late. His eyes met those of his assailant as the sharp blade sliced through soft skin, hard muscle, and even softer organs.

Jody groaned in pain right along with Zeke. She swore she could *feel* it. His stomach. The blade slit his stomach. The man's eyes were cold and merciless when he twisted the knife before pulling it out with a violent yank. The sound alone made Jody want to vomit.

"That should teach you to mind your own fucking business," the murderer threatened, spitting on Zeke as he fell to his knees.

Zeke's hands covered the stab wound, trying to stanch the flow of blood, but Jody knew it would only be a short time before there was no more blood to hold in. The villain took a step back, watching Zeke fall to the ground before running into the darkness. Jody lamented the lack of justice at Zeke's killer having gotten away. Hers and Zeke's attention was suddenly drawn to a figure materializing from the shadows.

"What happened?" the new man asked urgently as he guided Zeke to his back. "I'm a doctor."

"I got stabbed," Zeke croaked out.

"I can see that," the doctor acknowledged with a frown, staring down at the blood pooling beneath Zeke's fingers.

"I didn't think. I was trying to help a damsel in distress," Zeke admitted with a chuckle that turned into a cough accompanied by more blood.

"Shit," the doctor whispered, glancing down at the wound and back up into Zeke's eyes.

The look in the doctor's eyes told her everything. She'd seen it far too many times to count. Zeke didn't have long left. Jody felt ill knowing she was witnessing his last moments through his eyes. She didn't want to know what it felt like to die until it was her time. She didn't need to live the experience through someone else.

"I'm done, huh, Doc? At least I went down doing a good deed," Zeke mused, and Jody could tell he was smiling.

"You're a good man," the doctor acknowledged shaking his head, and Jody could clearly see indecision warring in his eyes.

What was he thinking? Why hadn't he called for an ambulance? Was he going to perform a mercy killing? Jody wished she could close her eyes, she couldn't watch.

Zeke lifted his blood-covered hand a looked at it. "Blood scares me."

"Fuck," the doctor cursed, and pulled at his hair. "Well, then you're going to hate this."

Jody watched an all-too familiar scene unfold where the doctor used fangs that suddenly appeared and drew them down his wrist, cutting into his veins and releasing blood of his own. His bloody wrist came closer to Zeke's face, and Jody had to imagine Zeke was in too much shock to protest. The familiar taste of blood registered with Jody and she knew Zeke was swallowing it down.

"You're too good of a man to let die like this," the doctor explained, shaking his head and pulling his wrist away.

"What? What's happening?" Zeke questioned in panic, looking down at where Jody could feel the wound closing.

"You'll be fine in a few hours. You better get out of here before the cops get here. I'll clean up the body," the doctor said.

"What body?" Zeke asked in confusion, sitting up.

Jody could feel the turmoil running through him. She knew that feeling, too ... she'd experienced it just days ago when trying to figure out what this new world was that had beings like the doctor who saved Zeke and what her place was in it.

The doctor smiled at Zeke, blood still clinging to the fangs. "Your attacker." The doctor turned to leave, then paused a moment before turning back. "Don't die anytime soon, otherwise you're going to have to get over that fear of blood pretty damned quick."

Zeke opened his mouth, presumably to ask another question, but the Vampire was gone.

Gasping for breath, Jody sat up straight in the bed. For a moment, she was disoriented. It took a few seconds to realize she wasn't *there*, she was still in Zeke's bed. Arms wrapped around her from behind and she fought off the panic and urge to lash out. He pulled her so she lay back down, this time, wrapped in his solid arms against his equally solid chest.

"You're safe," he whispered to her while running his hands down over her hair. "Go back to sleep."

How could she sleep after that? She assumed what she'd seen was another one of those dreams Zeke had said were really memories from his blood. He'd nearly *died*. Everything in her knew he *should* have died. The man giving him blood was obviously a

Vampire, and that's why he healed. She didn't want to close her eyes and see what other memories his blood conjured for her for today's macabre film festival.

"Always helping the damsel in distress, huh?" Jody whispered.

"Always. But I don't want to discuss it. I know what you saw, I don't need to relive it. Not now," Zeke refused, his tone conveying the finality of his request.

"How long will I have these?" she whispered, her eyelids already slipping closed of their own accord. The feeling of his fingers brushing along her scalp was too soothing to fight off.

"I don't know," Zeke's voice came from behind her, and she felt his shoulders rise and fall with a shrug. "But I will hold onto you so you remember it's not real." She could hear the smile in his voice. He was teasing her, she knew it, but she wasn't about to turn down his offer. She needed the support of those strong arms to face whatever else he already had.

Jody was really hoping for maybe a normal dream after the last blood memory. Or maybe something small like a papercut or one of Zeke as a kid stapling his finger, goodness knows every kid did that at least once during childhood. But she knew that wasn't what she would be getting.

Now that she'd seen a couple of them, Jody had started to recognize when she was in one. The pictures were clearer than a dream, like they were in sharper focus, and so were the sounds. It felt so much like being awake that if she wasn't aware she was asleep and in one of these memories, she might have actually thought she was living these out in the real world.

This one started off peaceful enough, no bad men assaulting women in parking lots. Zeke was driving a pickup truck, and through the windshield she could see snow falling rapidly in the illumination of the headlights. The flakes were big and fluffy, but were falling fast. A sinking sense of foreboding settled in Jody's gut. She knew what was going to happen. These memories adhered themselves to blood, which meant the peaceful drive through a near-blizzard was about to take a turn for the worst.

Zeke slowed the truck and stopped for a red light. Jody could make out the faint sounds of some kind of radio talk show murmuring in the background. She did the same thing when it was snowing; turned down the music, and reduced any distractions so she could concentrate better. Zeke dug around in the passenger seat, searching for something, and Jody wanted to yell at him to pay attention in front of him, even though he was stopped. Something was going to go wrong. When he finally turned his attention back to the road, the light was green and he immediately pressed on the gas. The truck was halfway through the intersection when movement from the corner of Zeke's eye caught his attention. He turned his head just in time to see a cube van slide through the intersection.

Jody could feel the panic flood Zeke's entire body, and he pressed on the gas pedal, attempting to make it through the intersection before the cube van made contact. The snow was greasy under the tires and didn't allow for much traction. Jody could see the terrified expression on the other driver's face when the two vehicles collided.

Pain and darkness. Those were the only two things that registered with Jody through the memory. Endless pain and endless darkness. They continued for an eternity and she tried to claw her way out, tried to make it stop. But it wasn't over.

Muffled yelling reached her ears through the memory. The voices became clearer, but what they said made no sense. The words are garbled and distorted. Zeke's eyes opened a crack, and through blurry vision Jody could see only abstract shapes resembling people. The people rushed around, and now Jody could make out individual features and colors. Blue. There was so much blue around her. She recognized the color—it was the same shade of the scrubs she wore at the hospital.

"We're losing him!" a clear voice finally pierced through the garble.

Deafening beeping noises drowned out all other sounds. The yelling of what Jody could see was obviously hospital staff merged together into one loud amalgamation that put more pressure on the pain she could feel in her head … Zeke's head. A face grew larger in her field of vision and she could make out the individual features. Jody's mind reared back from the image. She knew that face well. It was one she saw every day. When she looked in the mirror.

CHAPTER SEVENTEEN

"Oh my God!" Jody gasped.

Fighting for air, she tried to sit up, away from Zeke. She'd been there. She'd seen him die. Jody even *remembered* him. It was right before Thanksgiving; there had been a pretty bad snow storm, and she'd worked an extra shift at the hospital, figuring it would be less of a hassle than trying to get home in that crap and then drive back in a few hours. She had been needed, too. There had been quite a few accidents that night, but she remembered Zeke's.

He had been in really bad shape when they brought him in. The paramedics hadn't thought he'd make it through the drive from the scene. Obviously he had, but not much longer after that. They hadn't even gotten a full assessment of his injuries or gotten him into the OR before he was gone. Then, he was *gone.* Zeke's body disappeared from the morgue. There had been a big police investigation, and as a result an entirely new surveillance system had been installed in the whole facility.

"Jody?" Zeke questioned, his arm still wrapped around her.

"I saw you die!" she freaked out.

"It's okay, I'm here now. It was just another memory," his voice drifted soothingly from behind her where he still held her tight.

"No. I *saw* you die," Jody emphasized, attempting to get her frantic breathing under control. "I was *there.*"

"It's okay, princess," Zeke tried again.

"You don't understand. I was *there.* I was at the hospital. I watched you die. In real life," Jody agonized. She saw people die often, but it was entirely different when someone she watched flicker away was now holding her in his bed after having rescued her.

Zeke turned her so she was on her back and he hovered above her. His intimidating frame kept her body pinned in place and his dark eyes bored into hers.

"I thought you looked familiar," he whispered, brushing a strand of hair from her face and tucking it behind her ear. "I don't know how I could ever have forgotten your beautiful face."

His gaze wandered over her features, taking in each individual facet—her eyes, her nose, and then her mouth. He stayed focused on her mouth and his tongue emerged to wet his bottom lip absently. Jody could almost see the thoughts written on his face. He wanted to kiss her. Did she want that, too? It took her all of two seconds to decide she did, she most definitely did.

As if reading her thoughts, Zeke lowered his mouth to hers in a tentative kiss. When he moved to pull away, Jody wrapped a hand around his neck and pulled him back to her. She pressed her lips to his again, and what started as a shy and nervous kiss exploded in a fervent exchange. Zeke's weight settled deliciously over her body and Jody ran her hands down his muscled back; her fingers memorized every dip and valley that reminded her of the strength lying beneath the skin and how gently he handled her. When her hands reached his perfect ass, she couldn't help the itch her fingers had to squeeze the taut flesh.

Zeke pulled away, looking aghast. "Are you getting fresh with me?" he demanded, his face cracking into a smile that made Jody swoon a little bit on the inside.

Jody let out a laugh and then a squeal of surprise when he rolled them so she straddled his prone body.

"That position wasn't very fair, I can't admire you properly that way," he told her.

She wasn't about to complain. She got a nice view of his cut chest and dreamy biceps from this angle.

"Are all Vampires this built?" Jody queried, running her hands down over his arms—undoubtedly the sexiest part of a man.

"You've seen many Vampires naked, have you?" he questioned, his eyebrows raised.

"I haven't seen *any* Vampires naked," Jody countered, feeling saucy.

"We'll have to change that," Zeke offered with a confident smile. Then, his smile wavered. "If you want that."

Uncertainty clouded his bright smile and Jody felt her own falter. What was she doing? She'd just met this man ... Vampire ... whatever. This was so not like her; she didn't do quick and casual hookups. It took her months to feel comfortable being any kind of intimate with a man. But there was something different about Zeke, a chemistry she hadn't experienced with *anyone* before.

"Jody?" Zeke whispered, his nervous eyes searching hers.

She felt like a deer caught in the headlights of an oncoming semi-truck. Zeke gently gripped her hips and lifted, obviously with the idea of moving her away from him.

"I'm sorry, I shouldn't have—" he started.

"I want that. I want *you*," Jody interrupted before he could finish and before he could remove her from her perch atop him.

Zeke froze with his hands still at her hips, eyeing her warily like she might yell "psych!" at him and jump off. Instead, she grabbed the hem of her borrowed shirt and pulled it over her head. He sucked in a breath at the view of her exposed skin, and Jody watched his eyes dilate as they looked her over. Chill bumps raced across her skin in the open air and her nipples hardened under his appraisal. When he didn't move for a few moments, self-consciousness crept into Jody's mind. What did he see when he looked at her? She moved to cover her exposed breasts, but Zeke stopped her with gentle hands.

"Don't. I can see what you're thinking. You're absolutely gorgeous, Jody," he breathed out, shaking his head, his hair making dull scraping sounds against the pillowcase.

Jody felt her stomach do a little swoop. The admiring gleam in his eyes told her he meant every word. Bracing her hands on his hard chest, she leaned in to press her lips to his. Zeke wrapped an arm around her back and the other tangled in her hair where he kept her pressed against him. He swiped his tongue along her bottom lip, and Jody couldn't contain the needy moan erupting from her.

Her noises spurred him on, and within moments they were both stripped of their remaining clothing and their hands choreographed a frantic dance of caressing and groping, all the while their mouths never parted. Jody felt Zeke's sizable erection press between them and decided she was done with foreplay, she was ready for the featured attraction. Slipping a hand between them, she wrapped her fingers around Zeke's arousal. He let out a hiss and she smiled against his mouth. After a few strokes, she lifted her hips, placing his hard cock against her entrance. Zeke's grip on her hips tightened and she eased him inside. There were no more insecurities or doubts between them. This is what she wanted. This was what they *both* wanted.

Jody let out a moan of pleasure with every inch of Zeke that filled her. The stretch of the invasion after going so long without sex was positively delectable.

When he was fully seated inside of her, she pressed her hand against his chest.

"Just give me a second," she gasped.

Zeke held tight to her hips, but didn't make any moves, waiting for her to set the pace. After a moment, she began to work her hips up and down *very* slowly, still trying to get used to the feeling of a man inside her after so long. A brush of Zeke's finger over her clit sent a jolt through her and she threw back her head in ecstasy.

"Right there, just like that," she whispered when he found the right pressure and the right spot.

His pace kept time with hers—even and lazy strokes—but she needed more. Jody increased her pace and Zeke followed suit. Soon the quiet of the room was chased away by their collective moans of pleasure and the sound only flesh against flesh could make. Jody sped to a frantic pace, racing toward her climax. Her entire body stiffened and then shuddered when she plummeted over the cliff. A loud groan left her lips and she collapsed onto Zeke's chest.

"God, princess, that felt so good," he whispered into her sweat-dampened hair.

Jody didn't even have the energy to answer through her panting breaths. Zeke returned to pushing into her and drawing back out in a slow and steady rhythm. Somewhere in the back of her mind, she realized he hadn't come yet. She lifted her head from his chest—she got hers, now she was going to make sure he got his, too. No man would ever say she was a selfish lover.

"You going for another?" he asked with a smirk that made her lady parts clench.

Nodding, she gave her best sultry smile in return. She'd go for a second orgasm as long as he got one, too. Jody lifted her hips with shaking muscles and a whole lot of effort. Zeke chuckled, and in a blink she was flipped to her back. He hooked her ankles over his shoulders and slowly pushed into her, his eyes never leaving hers. His big hands grabbed onto her hips and angled them up toward him and Jody let out a gasp at the change in sensation. She could feel every push and drag along her g-spot.

"Touch yourself. Let me see how you play with that clit," he ordered.

Jody found her fingers complying of their own accord, surprised his commands sent a thrill through her. She'd never been one for being told what to do in the bedroom, but she had a sneaking suspicion she could definitely get into it with Zeke.

Within moments, she was back at the edge of the cliff, ready to dive over. She pulled her hand away, but Zeke grabbed her wrist and brought it back to her slick folds.

"Don't stop."

"I'm going to come," she whimpered, slowing the circling of her fingers to stave off plummeting.

"Come, princess. Let me see you come apart. You're so fucking beautiful," Zeke rambled, his thrusts faster and faster.

Jody obliged and brought herself to the edge again, and then dove over with a scream. She barely registered Zeke's answered shout. His weight when he collapsed onto her, however, was a little more difficult to ignore.

"Princess," Zeke murmured from where his face was pillowed between her breasts.

"Hmmm?" Jody answered sleepily. All the energy seemed to have been sapped from her body and all she wanted to do now was sleep.

"That was amazing," he boasted, lifting his head to gaze into her heavily-lidded eyes.

He pressed a kiss on her chest, just above her breast before shifting his weight off her. Jody sighed in relief when she could fully straighten her legs again. It wasn't exactly a contortionist act, but that was more stretching than she'd done in a long time. She was going to be sore in the morning. Or evening. Or whenever it was they were actually going to get up and leave the bed. All she knew was right now was not that time.

Zeke pulled her body toward his. Jody rolled to her side and froze when a wet trickle slid down her thigh. Her eyes went wide and she looked up at Zeke in panic. How stupid could she be? They hadn't used any kind of protection.

"What happened? Are you all right?" Zeke asked, his attention focused solely on her.

"We didn't use a condom," Jody whispered, afraid saying it louder might encourage the worst case scenario to happen.

"Oh, shit. I'm sorry, I didn't even think," Zeke panicked, jumping from the bed and pacing back and forth in front of her.

"Hey, um, I'm on birth control, so we should be okay. I mean, birth control isn't one hundred percent effective, but the chances are pretty slim," she replied calmly after her brain started kicking back to life after her momentary freak out—she'd almost forgotten she had a vaginal ring contraceptive in.

Zeke let out a huge breath and fell backward onto his back on the bed.

"I'm sorry I freaked you out, I've just never had sex without a condom before," she explained, looking down between her legs. "I forgot it might be, um, messy. I'm going to go clean up."

Closing herself in the bathroom, Jody cleaned up, chiding herself for being careless, but also for being a spaz about what was essentially a non-issue. She supposed that's what happened when people got caught up in the passion of the moment—forgetfulness.

When she returned to Zeke's room, she pulled the shirt she'd borrowed from him over her head and chewed on her lip while contemplating whether she should crawl back into bed with him. Did he want her to? Would it be weird if she did? Would it be weird if she *didn't*?

Zeke flipped the covers in invitation, answering at least one of her questions. Jody crawled into bed, and he pulled her so her back was pressed against his chest.

"I never meant to put you at risk," he murmured in her ear.

Jody didn't quite know how to respond to that, so she just nodded. Within moments, Zeke's deep breathing lulled her to sleep right alongside him.

CHAPTER EIGHTEEN

When Jody awoke at dusk, it was in a far less alarming manner than the last time waking in Zeke's bed, albeit this time was a little more awkward. The feeling of something hard pressing into her hip brought consciousness to the forefront of her mind, as did the realization her face was tucked under his chin and snuggled up to his chest.

"Morning, princess," Zeke's deep voice rumbled through her, her core clenching at the timbre.

"I think, technically, it's evening," she corrected with a yawn.

Peeking her head up, Jody peered at the clock on Zeke's dresser. Yep. Just after six thirty in the evening. They'd slept the entire day and yet she still felt exhausted. She gave herself a pep talk to get out of bed, but that method never worked for her before, so there was no reason it should now. With working such inconsistent hours at the hospital, she usually needed at least two, sometimes three alarms to get her out of bed and was in a perpetual state of exhaustion most times.

Tentatively, she stuck her foot out from under the covers, knowing the air would be cold. It was the equivalent of sticking a toe in the water to test the temperature when she *knew* it was going to be freezing. It would have been faster and a lot easier if she just whipped the covers off and steeled herself for the frigid temperatures—like ripping off a Band-Aid.

"Where do you think you're going?" Zeke asked, a note of playfulness in his voice.

"I need to get up, I've been in bed all day," Jody answered, pulling away from the warmth of Zeke's body. A little whimper sounded in the back of her mind at the loss of his heat, and she tried to shush it away.

"It's cold out there, isn't there anything I can do to convince you to stay?" Zeke's voice rumbled again; this time the playfulness was replaced with unmistakable need.

Hearing the desire in his voice spiked her own. Jody didn't *really* want to get out of the bed. It was cold out there and warm under the covers next to Zeke. There wasn't much of a contest here. Snuggling closer to Zeke's chest, she gave a little sigh of contentment when her skin made contact with his. Zeke's hand glided down her back and then up under her shirt. The feeling of his warm hand and soft touch sent a shiver through her.

"I think I need you to warm me up," Jody breathed out, pressing a kiss to his bare chest.

"I can definitely do that," Zeke groaned.

His hand traveled down her back to knead one of her cheeks, the contact sending a wave of arousal through her. Jody slung her leg over his hip, giving him permission to explore farther. Zeke's fingers slowly trailed down to the back of her thighs before slipping between them. She let out a moan when he brushed against her bare folds. He teased her, lightly brushing along her labia, for a few moments before she pushed her hips back toward his hand, begging for more.

A single finger slid through the gathering moisture toward her entrance, but he bypassed it in favor of seeking out her clit. With measured movements, he stroked along the engorged nub, bringing Jody closer and closer to climax. In a sudden flurry of movement, he flipped them so she lay on his chest, her thighs spread wantonly open for him.

"Why'd you stop?" Jody panted, peering up at him in confusion.

Zeke silenced her with a scorching kiss before sliding a finger inside of her. A few thrusts later, Jody found herself on her back with him hovering above her. Knowing he could move her like she weighed nothing sent a thrill through her. She'd never had a lover who took what he wanted, but gave so much in return.

"I need to taste you," he murmured through kisses trailed down over her shirt.

Jody made quick work of removing the barrier between her skin and his lips, tossing the shirt across the room. Cold be damned … she had Zeke to keep her warm. Zeke chuckled at her desperate movements, but continued his journey southward, placing a reverent kiss on the top of her mound before running his tongue through her slick folds.

"Oh, God," Jody whispered, kneading her breasts.

Zeke continued his ministrations with fervor, and all Jody could do was make desperate groans and whimpers to show her appreciation. There were no words that could express the pleasure Zeke drew from her with his attentions. Pressure built low within her and she was moments away from exploding.

"I'm going to come," she warned through a groan.

"Come, princess," he ordered against her over-sensitized skin.

Even without the command, Jody would have plummeted over the edge. White lights flashed behind her eyes and she let out a cry she would never have recognized as her own. The white faded to gray and tugged in black toward the edges of her vision.

"I think I'm going to pass out," she mumbled, her eyelids too heavy to open.

Zeke chuckled. "That good, huh?"

Jody could only nod. The haze began to clear and so did the frantic sound of blood pumping filling her ears.

"You want another?" Zeke offered, brushing a finger down her center and causing her whole body to jolt, even when she thought she could no longer move. She could hear the gloating smile in his voice.

He definitely deserved to gloat. She wondered how many other men could say they nearly made a woman pass out by giving them an orgasm with just their tongue.

"I think I need a minute," Jody gasped out, still trying to catch her breath.

Jody smiled sleepily at him while he trailed kisses back up her body. He hesitated above her mouth. She'd never been a big fan of tasting herself after a guy had gone down on her, but she would get past that in a heartbeat if it meant she could get a taste of Zeke's lips. Wrapping a languid arm around the back of his neck, she pulled him in for a deep kiss. She could taste her musky flavor on his tongue and found it did nothing to quell her desire for him.

"These. Off. Now," she panted, pulling at the waistband of his boxer briefs.

"As you wish, princess," he laughed. Jody's heart did a flip. Now he was quoting *The Princess Bride* to her? All kinds of swooning.

Zeke slipped his underwear off and threw them across the room somewhere to mingle with the shirt she'd already discarded.

"Where do you want me?" he asked, taking the line she was just about to utter.

Jody turned so she was planted firmly on her hands and knees. Looking back over her shoulder at him, the hunger in his eyes was unmistakable as he took in the view of her on all fours.

"I like it this way," she confessed, feeling wanton for pretty much the first time in her life.

"Fuck, princess," he breathed out, running his hand over the curve of her ass and giving it a healthy squeeze.

"Yes, please," Jody whispered, and gave him what she hoped was a sultry smile. Along with never having been wanton before she was pretty sure she'd never been sultry before either.

Groaning, Zeke stroked his hardness a few times before lining up at her entrance. He paused there for a moment, and Jody was nearly positive she would die from the anticipation if he didn't fill her immediately.

"Please," she begged, another first for her in bed.

Pushing her hips backward, Jody hoped to encourage him. Zeke obliged and slid inside of her slick channel in one thrust. They let out a collective moan when his hips made contact with her flesh. He thrust in and out slowly a few times and Jody pushed her hips back toward him, urging him to go faster. Gripping her hips, he quickened his pace, giving her exactly what she needed. She dropped her head to the pillow and let out a moan at the change in angle. It hit all the right spots, and now she was already close to another orgasm. Jody stroked between her thighs, searching for another cliff to dive from; it was just up ahead, not far at all. Zeke squeezed both cheeks at once and it sent her flying over the edge. Jody mumbled unintelligible words or curses—she had no recollection which—into the pillow. Zeke stilled behind her with his responding release.

Jody stayed frozen in place with her ass in the air, even after Zeke had separated their bodies. She wasn't even sure she had enough strength to move to lay down where her neck wasn't being bent at an awkward angle. Zeke carefully laid her on her side and she laughed.

"What's so funny?" Zeke asked, smiling down at her.

"I bet I look so ridiculous," she said, laughing again.

"Ridiculous isn't the word I would use. Incredibly sexy is more like it," he growled, pulling her against his body and kissing down her neck. Somehow his coordination was much better than hers and he even managed to pull the comforter over them. "That was amazing."

"Best sex you've ever had?" Jody asked nervously, half teasing, half brimming with self-doubt.

"Absolutely." He reached around to cup one of her breasts.

"You're not just saying that?" she mumbled into the pillow.

"No, I'm not just saying that," Zeke replied adamantly.

"Good."

There was an emotional attachment starting to form between her and Zeke. At least on her end. Now Jody was terrified she was going to get hurt. Maybe it was a better idea to put some distance between them.

"I need a shower," she announced in the quiet room.

Before he could get a word out, she leapt from the bed and headed toward the bathroom.

"Princess," Zeke called out, his voice both filled with concern and warning. He definitely knew she was freaking out.

"I'll be out in a few," Jody reassured, looking at him over her shoulder, trying to give him her best *I'm totally fine* smile and failing.

The sight of him lying in the bed with the comforter tucked under his arm gave a nice view of his sculpted arms and chest. A little shiver of arousal ran through Jody just looking at him.

Space. She definitely needed some space that wasn't occupied by all his sexiness.

CHAPTER NINETEEN

Scrambling into the shower, Jody's heart beat a frantic staccato. She'd totally lost track of her purpose the moment she'd climbed into Zeke's bed. This wasn't some fledgling relationship they were building on; this was a case of damsel in distress meets knight in shining armor. And this damsel completely forgot there was a sister in a similar situation out there. It had been nice, however, to just forget about her problems and that of her sister and pretend she was in a real fairytale where the knight or prince—or in this case, Vampire—rescued her from danger and she could live happily ever after. Not that she'd been thinking about a happy ever after with Zeke. Not really. Okay, she was alone with her thoughts, was there really too much harm in admitting there was a little spark of hope that this short amount of time they'd spent together—with phenomenal sex, she had to add—would turn into something more? Yes, yes there was. Because he was a *Vampire*. He hadn't done anything Vampire-y to her, like bite her or anything, but he was still one. A hot one. Why did he have to be so hot? And sweet? And a fantastic lover? And just … amazing?

Closing her eyes, Jody tilted her head back, letting the warm spray of water beat down on her face. Maybe it would beat some sense into her. She was pining after a *Vampire*, for crying out loud. How would that ever work? I mean, look at *Twilight* ... Bella wound up a Vampire in the end. *Vampire Diaries*? Once again, the girl ended up a Vampire. Jody wasn't too keen on the idea of being a Vampire. These weren't even thoughts she should be having. She barely knew Zeke. But what she did know put him in the category of damn-near perfect. She just couldn't help herself from going through the what-ifs. She just wished she could talk to Alicia about it; she always seemed to be so level-headed with men.

An idea struck Jody nearly off her feet. *Of course!* She may not have a phone, and neither did Zeke, but that didn't mean they couldn't get to their contacts. Slapping the water off, Jody stumbled out of the shower in her hurry to get to Zeke to tell him her epiphany. She ripped the towel she'd used after her last shower off the hook on the wall and dried herself haphazardly.

"Zeke!" she called, running out of the bathroom toward his bedroom.

"Princess?" his voice came from the kitchen.

"Do you have a laptop? We might not have our phones, but we can get to our contacts through Google!" she yelled as she cantered down the hall.

"What?" he asked when she rounded the corner into the kitchen.

Hot. Damn. Jody skidded to a halt at the sight of a shirtless Zeke cooking for her. Again. Why did he have to be so fucking perfect … aside from the Vampire part? She was starting to think she could totally get past the blood-drinking thing if she could keep him.

"I couldn't understand you, what?" Zeke asked, turning to face her.

His jaw nearly hit the floor as he took in her towel-clad state. His eyes turned hungry as they roamed over her. Jody swallowed thickly. There was definitely irrepressible chemistry between them. No matter how much she tried to douse the flames, they seemed to linger as embers until they were in the same room again, then it was like adding gasoline and she had to step back from the white-hot heat.

"Damn, princess," Zeke growled, his voice turned husky.

"Wh–what are you working on there?" Jody was going for nonchalance, trying to diffuse some of tension with the stupid question. It was obvious what he was doing.

Zeke pointed to the clock. "Spaghetti. You haven't eaten for hours."

"Uh, do you need to go out and *eat* again?" Jody asked, wincing.

She would have thought that little exchange would have snuffed out her desire, but of course not.

"No. There's only one thing here I want." He looked her up and down, and there was an unmistakable predatory glint in his eyes.

Jody felt her eyes go wide. Okay, well there was the Vampire-iness she was worried about.

Zeke's gaze turned from heated to shocked realization. "That came out wrong. I wasn't …" He hung his head and barked out a little laugh. "I didn't mean your blood. I meant I want *you*. In bed. Again."

When Jody didn't move or speak, he twisted back to the stove and stirred the spaghetti. Then he turned back to her slowly and a smirk graced his lips.

"Well, that went downhill pretty quick," he observed with an embarrassed laugh. "I guess I need to work on my lines. So, what were you saying earlier before I made a complete ass of myself?"

Zeke leaned back against the counter with his arms crossed over his chest. Jody couldn't help but stare at the way his biceps bulged in that flexed position.

How? she chastised herself. How could she still want him after she thought he was going to eat her? Groaning inwardly at her stupid hormones, she took a deep breath to clear her thoughts. All that did was invite the enticing aroma of the spaghetti he was cooking— entirely *for her*, because he didn't eat—into her lungs. If she could have slapped herself without looking completely insane, she would have.

"You all right there, princess?" he asked, pushing away from the counter and walking toward her, a concerned frown on his face.

Jody's brain kicked into gear. If he touched her, she was a goner. They'd end up right back in his bed.

"Yeah. I was saying earlier," she started out slowly, not trusting she wouldn't trip over her own tongue or a stream of drool wouldn't come cascading down her chin, "if you have a computer, we should be able to get to your contacts from Google. If you have an Android device, that is. Had. I guess it's had now, isn't it?" she heard herself ramble.

Zeke had stopped about a foot from her and she forced herself to look up at him. He worried his bottom lip between his teeth and then let out a huge sigh. Without touching her, he took a cautious step backward. When he was back at his post leaning against the counter, he rubbed his hand across the back of his neck.

"No, I don't have a computer. It was in my truck when it got totaled, and I haven't really needed one since," he answered with a shrug. "You're scared of me, aren't you?" The sudden question startled Jody.

"A little." She regretted her honesty immediately when his face fell. "But not like you think," she added quickly.

"Oh?" Zeke asked, eyebrows raised.

"This is going to sound crazy. I know it will." Jody laughed, sounding a little insane for sure now. "I'm not scared of what you are, I'm scared of how you make me feel," she confessed, carefully enunciating each word so it permeated into not only his brain, but her own.

"How do I make you feel, princess?" he inquired, his face betraying his confusion.

"Like I want impossible things." Jody let out a nervous laugh, then shook her head. "I told you it was going to sound crazy."

"What impossible things?" he pressed, and Jody wanted to kick herself for saying anything at all. Of course she couldn't just say something enigmatic like that and expect him to walk away.

"Oh God," she groaned, covering her face with her hands. "I'm just going to sound like some love-struck rescued damsel in distress. Is there a name for that syndrome?"

When Zeke didn't answer she continued with nervous rambling to fill the silence, "Things with you. I like you. I mean, how are you still single? You're like the perfect man. Errr, Vampire, whatever. But I don't even know if you'd want that. Or that *I* really want that. I mean, how would that work? You're a Vampire, I'm a human. In all the books, the girl who loves the Vampire ends up being one herself. Not that I *love* you, I don't even really know you. Oh, God. I'm just going to shut up now."

When at least a small fraction of mortification from her proverbial word vomit subsided, Jody hazarded a look at Zeke. He stood directly in front of her again, though she hadn't heard him move. Perks of being a deadly predator, she guessed. A goofy smile was plastered on his face.

"You like me?" he asked, his smile widening to brighten his whole face, and my oh my was the sight glorious.

"Well, if that's all you heard and ignored the rest, then that's fine by me." Jody sighed, and then erupted in a fit of giggles.

Zeke pulled her still towel-clad body into his arms, and she felt the most profound sense of comfort and relief at his embrace. Here, pressed to his solid body, she felt safe. The irony of feeling safe encaged by a Vampire's arms was not lost on her.

"I like you, too," he admitted, the words rumbling through his chest to her ear pressed against it. "Let's figure out how to find Jackson and your sister first, then we'll figure out us."

Butterflies erupted in Jody's stomach at the word *us*.

"But neither of us have phones, and you don't have a computer," Jody pointed out, trying to get her brain back to working through their problem instead of creating new ones.

"We could go to the library," Zeke offered.

Jody pulled away from him and gave a bright smile. "You're brilliant!"

Zeke pointed to the clock on the microwave. It read ten thirty. At night. "We'll have to wait until tomorrow."

Groaning, Jody rested her forehead on his chest. "Okay, tomorrow," she relented.

"Let's get you fed. And dressed ... although, I'm not going to complain about your current choice of attire." His eyes traveled to where the towel barely covered her breasts.

She couldn't help but laugh. "Clothes first," she amended his earlier plan, "then food."

When Jody returned to the kitchen, she was positively beaming. How was it possible to feel so happy when everything outside Zeke's little house was shit? The sight of Zeke plating her spaghetti gave her more butterflies. What was it about a man who cooked for her that gave her heart palpitations?

"What would you like to do with the rest of our night?" Zeke queried, sliding into a chair across the table from her.

Jody glanced over at the clock; it was just a few minutes shy of eleven o'clock. She wasn't exactly a stranger to odd hours, but she didn't know if her body would allow her to stay up the entire night like she was sure Zeke did.

"Not all night," Zeke clarified. "Just a little while until your stomach settles."

Nodding, Jody shoveled a forkful of the pasta into her mouth. She had to stifle a moan and close her eyes to keep them from rolling into the back of her head. This spaghetti was *nothing* like the frozen stuff in the little plastic trays which were the only thing she had time to cook.

"Is it all right?" Zeke questioned, but there was no worry in his voice, only a note of smug triumph. Oh, he knew damned well it was delicious.

"This is amazing," Jody answered when her mouth was no longer filled.

"It was my mom's recipe," he answered, somewhat wistfully.

"Did you do a lot of cooking, before, you know?" Jody pried, not sure how sensitive he might be talking about his past. It felt awkward to her to ask the getting to know you kinds of questions *after* she'd already slept with him. She'd never done it in that order before.

"I used to be a chef," he recalled with a wink.

Oh, that wink did wicked things to her lady-parts.

"Of course you were," Jody chuckled, taking another bite of her pasta. Rich tomato flavor paired exquisitely with herbs filled her mouth and she wasn't sure she would get enough even once her plate was empty.

"How about a movie after dinner?" he offered.

It felt almost like a real date with dinner and a movie to follow ... if she ignored the fact she was the only one eating and was holed up in a Vampire's house because there were *other* Vampires out there who wanted to kill her. And probably eat her. This felt so normal in the face of everything from the last few days.

"A movie sounds great," Jody answered after she swallowed down another mouthful of bliss.

"What do you like?" Zeke eagerly leaned forward on the table.

"Pretty much anything," she remarked with a shrug. It was true, for the most part. "You can pick. I call the right to veto, though. Choose your favorite," she encouraged with a grin. She'd love to see what he picked.

"All right, you asked for it," he warned with a little bounce of his eyebrows.

Zeke disappeared into the living room and Jody took the time to survey the kitchen. It was all white walls and empty countertops. No little touches to show it belonged to somebody.

"How long have you lived here?" Jody called to him from the kitchen. She was pretty sure she didn't need to yell that loud; he seemed to have a fairly acute sense of hearing.

"It's a rental. I've been here a couple months." He appeared in the doorway, holding his chosen movie behind his back. "I had to assume a whole new identity," he added, answering her unspoken question.

It made sense he would, he'd died in view of a dozen or more people in the hospital. They'd filed paperwork. As far as the authorities were concerned, he was dead and his body had been stolen away for some sinister purpose. It made sense in her brain, but it made her sad, too. It was a kind of bittersweet sadness, though. He'd died and would have lost everything anyway, but this way he got to make a fresh start and he was still *here*.

"What did you pick?" Jody asked, choking back her tears.

"Hey, now," Zeke crooned softly, kneeling at her feet. He caught the tears she'd been trying to hold back on his thumbs and wiped them away. "It's not all that bad," he comforted. "My movie collection is actually pretty good considering I've been picking them up from second-hand shops."

Jody let out a watery laugh and he gave her a sad smile in return. At least he seemed to have a sense of humor about everything and took this new life in stride. She wasn't so sure she could have done the same. It was a lot to take in.

Holding up the movie, Zeke presented it to her as though they were the crown jewels and she couldn't help but laugh.

"Are you sure you really want to watch that?" she questioned carefully. Of all the movies out there, he'd picked *Blade*.

"You said to pick my favorite. So here it is. Wesley Snipes in all his glory ... a kick-ass Vampire fighting the bad Vampires," Zeke elaborated, looking scandalized that she would question his choice in movies. "I'm not a day-walker, but this is kind of like what I do at night," he revealed, glancing down at the cover of the DVD case.

Jody scrunched her eyebrows together. When Zeke saw her look of confusion, he stood and held out his hand to her. She took it without hesitation and followed him into the living room. He led her to the couch and left her there while he put in the movie. Jody made herself comfortable while he pressed buttons and the TV flickered to life. When he returned to the couch, he took the seat next to her and pulled her so her head rested on his shoulder.

"At night, when I'm hunting, I'm going after the bad guys, Jody," he explained, his eyes glued to the TV. "Sick fuckers like the one who stabbed me when Jackson first saved me. Sometimes I go after other Vampires who have gotten out of hand. I want you to know I'm not a bad guy, princess. But I'm not a good guy either. I'm something ... in between," he finished, grinding his teeth.

Jody reached a hand up and turned his face toward her. "I know you're not a bad guy," she comforted, staring into his eyes. "And no one is all good."

"You are," he whispered. "I shouldn't even be here with you like this."

"No one is all good," she repeated adamantly.

She would not let him believe he was not worthy of her. He may still be in this world because of dark forces of some kind, but that didn't make him a monster.

Closing his eyes, Zeke rested his forehead against hers. Jody placed a tentative kiss on his lips. He seemed to savor it for a moment before taking control of it. Hungrily, he devoured her mouth and their movie was forgotten. Jody didn't need to watch it, anyway; she hadn't told him, but it was one of her favorites, too.

When the ending credits scrolled across the screen Jody giggled to herself. They'd spent the better part of an hour and a half making out on the couch like a couple of teenagers. In a way she was glad there was no sex, it felt more like a first date that way.

"Something funny there, princess?" Zeke challenged, scooping her up in his arms.

"I just felt like a teenager again, that's all," Jody laughed while he carried her down the hallway to his bedroom.

Zeke huffed. "Not me, I never made out with a girl as hot as you when I was a teenager."

Jody covered her mouth with a hand to stifle another giggle. But Zeke pulled her hand away and replaced it with his lips. Her body fell into the fluffy cloud that was his comforter and she let out a contented sigh. It was just too bad they had to face reality in the morning.

"Where did you go?" Zeke whispered before trailing kisses down her neck.

She sighed. "I was just thinking about how morning brings about reality."

Zeke planted another kiss on her lips before shedding his clothing and crawling into bed next to her. Jody snuggled into his warm body and breathed in the scent that was solely Zeke's. Clean and at the same time so manly. It reminded her of hiking through the woods after a rainstorm—green and robust, but with the hint of wet earth. It was her favorite smell in the world next to baking cookies.

"'Night, princess," Zeke whispered before pressing a kiss to the top of her head.

"'Night, knight," she answered, giggling at her own pun. She definitely needed sleep when she started laughing at her own jokes.

Zeke snorted but then his breathing turned steady and rhythmic, just like the heart beating beneath her hand on his chest.

CHAPTER TWENTY

It was another one of those blood memories, dammit. Jody could tell right away. She didn't particularly like them very much, since … well, they involved blood. But on the flipside, they gave her a better glimpse into the man Zeke was before and the Vampire he was now.

A light blanket of snow covered the ground as he crunched across it, and Jody could feel the tremors wracking his body. Pain shot through Zeke's foot and Jody got the distinct pleasure of experiencing every jolt. When he directed his gaze down, Jody gasped when she saw bare feet. And bare legs. And bare arms. And bare everything. Zeke was naked outside in the Minnesota wintertime and he would not last long. He continued to trudge through the snow, shivering and presumably ignoring the pain lancing through his feet with each step. It seemed he walked for hours—and maybe he had—when he came to a parking lot Jody recognized from a previous memory. This was the place he had been stabbed and the other Vampire, Jackson, had helped him.

Zeke circled the parking lot then stopping beside the building. He hadn't been there for more than a minute before another figure emerged from the darkness outside the ring of illumination of that lone light. Relief poured through Zeke that Jody could feel, and he fell to his knees.

"What h-happened to m-me?" Zeke stammered to the oncoming figure.

"Aw, fuck," Jackson swore, taking in Zeke's state. "What's the last thing you remember?" He pulled Zeke to his feet.

"An ac-accident and then the h-hospital," Zeke's teeth chattered. Jackson shrugged out of his jacket and laid it across Zeke's shoulders. "I w-was in the f-f-fucking m-morgue!"

"Come on, my truck is this way. Can you walk?" Jackson asked, looking down doubtfully at Zeke's bloody feet. "Never mind, wait here. I'll be right back."

Jackson disappeared back into the darkness and Jody could hear the sound of a vehicle starting before crunching gravel met her ears. A minute later, a truck pulled up next to Zeke and Jackson hopped out. He helped Zeke up into the passenger seat, then closed the door behind him.

When Jackson appeared in the driver's seat, he kept silent as he pulled the truck out of the parking lot. Zeke stared out the window, his shivering starting to subside.

"You died," Jackson stated, breaking into the silence.

"Am I like you now?" Zeke questioned, a note of hysteria edging into his voice.

"Yes," Jackson sighed, then ran his hand down his face.

"What am I?" Zeke followed up.

"A Vampire," Jackson replied simply, looking over at Zeke with furrowed brows.

Zeke took deep breaths, but Jody could still feel panic radiating from him.

The scene went dark after that, but another soon filled its place. From what Jody could tell, it was Zeke's first kill. She wished she could turn away, but that wasn't how these memories worked, apparently. She did take some solace in seeing Jackson in the background, guiding and keeping things in check. For some reason it made her feel better knowing Jackson was there as a mentor. Which also made her feel better knowing Jackson was protecting Alicia. This Jackson guy seemed to be good people, so knowing Alicia was with him put Jody's mind at ease. A little, anyway.

The rest of the night was a restless blur of Zeke helping damsels in distress, dudes in distress, and decapitating a few Vampires. By the time Jody woke in the morning, she had seen more blood and gore in her sleep than she saw in a whole month in the emergency room. And that was saying something.

Bright sunlight stabbed Jody in the eye, waking her from her not so restful sleep. Glaring at the curtains covering the window, she was tempted to growl. There was just the tiniest sliver of light peeking through, and of course it was right across her face—nowhere else in the room, just directly over her eye. Carefully extricating herself from Zeke's grip, she padded over to cinch closed the offending drapery. On her way back to climb in the warm embrace of Zeke's arms, she chanced a glance at the clock. It was just after seven. Libraries opened at like eight, right?

Instead of heading to where she longed to go— next to the heater that was Zeke's body—Jody detoured to the bathroom instead, arguing with herself she'd end up having to pee anyway now that her body had woken up. When she finished up, her stomach made an embarrassingly loud grumble she was sure Zeke had heard in his sleep from the other room.

Tiptoeing back to Zeke's room, Jody found him still passed out, his mouth slightly ajar and looking so at peace. She watched the steady rise and fall of his chest for a moment before her stomach gave another growl. Not wanting to wake him with her impatient hunger, she carefully backed out of the room and pulled the door shut behind her.

In the kitchen she set to work making scrambled eggs and toast. When the eggs had finished cooking, she divided them in half and slid them onto two plates and popped a piece of toast on each. Jody hummed quietly to herself as she brought the plates to the table. Her plate-filled hands hovered over the table for a moment before she remembered he didn't eat. A noise in the doorway caught her attention and she found Zeke, clad in only his boxer briefs, leaned against the doorway watching her.

"I forgot," she startled, looking stupidly at the two plates clutched in her hands.

Zeke smiled sweetly at her and pushed off the doorframe. Taking the plates from her hands, he set them on the table.

"Thank you for making me breakfast." He framed her face with his hands, pressing a kiss to her lips.

"But you're not even going to eat it," Jody lamented, trying to look down at the plates.

Zeke held her face firm and stared into her eyes. "It doesn't matter. I love that you made me breakfast," he stressed with another kiss.

Jody gave him a coy smile and he kissed her forehead.

"Eat your eggs, I'm going to get some clothes on," he announced before releasing her.

"Oh, I wish you wouldn't," she blurted out, then covered her mouth with her hand.

Zeke let out a laugh and shook his head. "You're insatiable, princess."

"Only when it's you," she replied with a smirk.

That broadened his smile. "I'm glad Jackson called me," he confessed with a warm look.

"Me too." Jody smiled.

When Zeke left the room, Jody dug into her eggs. Then finished off his. There was no sense in letting perfectly good scrambled eggs go to waste. Feeling like she might have to roll out of the kitchen after two plates of eggs, she made her way to Zeke's bedroom to dress. She'd expected to find him in there, but the room was empty. She contemplated putting her own clothes back on, but decided she rather liked the loungy comfort of wearing Zeke's oversized sweats.

Once dressed, Jody peered in each room as she made her way through the house, trying to locate her hot Vampire. That was dangerous. He wasn't *hers*. They hadn't made anything official yet. It had been an encouraging conversation the day before where it *sounded* like maybe he was willing to try to work something out once they cleared up this mess with Alicia.

"Zeke?" she called once she made a full lap of the small house.

A loud knock on the kitchen window startled her, making her jump nearly out her skin. Jody held a hand over her heart while a smiling Zeke waved to her from outside.

"What are you doing? You almost gave me a heart attack!" she yelled at him through the glass.

He let out a hearty laugh she could hear through the panes. It was one of those full-on head-thrown back laughs. Jody couldn't help but smile back at him. A moment later he was gone from her sight and she heard boots stomping outside the door leading from the kitchen to outside. The door swung open and in came Zeke, along with a rush of cold air.

"I started the truck," he answered, gesturing to the truck behind him with his thumb. He brushed the remainder of the snow from his coat and closed the door. "I wanted to make sure it was warm for you."

Jody swooned a little ... again. She seemed to be in a constant state of swoon when he was around.

"Such a gentleman," she crooned with a shy smile.

"Anything for you, princess," Zeke replied with a grin.

See, there was more swooning. And butterflies ... lots of them.

"Shall we?" he offered, taking on a horrid accent Jody was sure was supposed to be British.

Jody scrambled into her boots and coat and took his proffered elbow.

"Watch out, the steps are still a little icy. I ran out of salt," he explained while keeping a tight grip on her arm.

He wasn't kidding. Jody slipped on the first step, tripped down the second, and landed in a nice set of big strong arms. Zeke chuckled and pulled her closer. Oh, she could live there forever. Damn her sister and her urgent need for help.

"I gotcha, princess." He set her on the solid and not-so-icy driveway. Zeke led her to the passenger side of the truck and boosted her up, his hands giving her butt a little squeeze on the way up.

"Hey!" Jody scolded in mock outrage.

"I just couldn't resist," he told her, completely unapologetically, which she was okay with. It was a nice change of pace to find someone who found her irresistible.

Another minute later, they were on the road toward the library. Zeke made a series of turns and Jody only new what direction they were headed because of the position of the sun. She'd never been through this neighborhood before, but it looked like Zeke knew where he was going. It was a good thing too, because she relied heavily—probably *too* heavily—on the navigation on her phone to get her places.

"Here we are," Zeke announced, pulling into a tiny parking lot next to a brick building that definitely screamed 'library' to Jody.

Zeke seemed to listen for a moment before a frown appeared on his face.

"What is it?" Jody panicked, looking around for danger.

"I don't hear anything. There are no other cars here either. I don't think it's open yet," he observed, turning to her.

Jody sighed. It was almost eight thirty in the morning, shouldn't libraries be open by now?

"I'll go check the hours," she announced, reaching for the door handle. Zeke's hand covered hers before she realized he was unbuckled and across the cab of the truck.

"I'll go, you stay here."

"Ooookay," Jody said slowly. Was there some kind of danger lurking out there he wasn't telling her about?

Zeke smiled reassuringly at her. "It's cold and icy. And I'm trying to be a gentleman," he explained with a chuckle.

Jody supposed that made sense. She nodded and his hand eased up over hers, but gave a little squeeze before he fully let go.

"Be right back," he announced and hopped from the cab. A moment later he returned, a sour expression on his face. "Winter hours say they don't open until eleven."

"What?" Jody yelled. "It's winter, in Minnesota. You would think they would be open *more* hours to give people something to do and a reason to get out of the house."

Zeke chuckled. "What do you want to do while we wait?"

Jody groaned. She was tired of waiting, she just wanted to make sure Alicia was all right and let her sister know *she* was all right. She needed a new phone.

That's it! A new phone.

"Zeke!" she yelled, which sounded much too loud in the small confines of the truck cab.

"Yes, princess," he answered carefully to her too-wide smile, like she was just about to lose it.

"We need to find a phone store. Or a store with phones. Someplace with phones. I don't have my wallet or ID, so I can't actually *buy* a new one, but they have *phones* there and *internet*," she emphasized, practically bouncing up and down in her seat.

"I follow." Zeke threw the truck in reverse and pulled out of the library parking lot. "There's a store a few miles away," he explained as he navigated slowly back through the labyrinth of icy streets.

Jody watched the houses as they drove past, admiring how pristine everything looked with the new coat of snow. A big complex of brick buildings came into view and Jody's heart stopped for a second before she could register what she saw.

"Stop!" she yelled to Zeke, slapping his arm with one hand and pointing out the window with the other.

"What is it?" Zeke demanded, immediately alert, clearly trying to figure out what the hell she was freaking out about.

"That's Alicia's car!" Jody exclaimed, pointing toward the building.

CHAPTER TWENTY-ONE

"Are you sure?" Zeke asked doubtfully.

Jody could see how he would question her. There were a lot of cars in the world that looked like Alicia's, except for one tiny detail Jody would recognize anywhere.

"I'm positive. See the Jack and Sally from *The Nightmare Before Christmas* on the back window? I got her that for Christmas. She hates those stick figure decals everyone puts on their cars that tells everyone precisely how many people and pets are in their family. So I got her one of those as a joke," Jody reasoned, jabbing her pointed finger toward Alicia's car.

Zeke threw the truck in reverse and pulled around the block. Jody could see a few other vehicles parked there, and one was a truck she recognized from Zeke's memories.

"That's Jackson's truck, isn't it?" she asked excitedly.

Zeke pulled into the tiny parking lot. Jody wasn't even sure it was *supposed* to be a parking lot. It looked more like the back entrance where the dumpsters were housed.

"Hey, I know this place," Jody recalled, looking at the building more closely. "This used to be a maternity hospital back in the day. I suppose it makes sense they would be in a medical facility if Alicia is working her engineering mojo on something."

Jody reached for the door handle, but Zeke stopped her.

"Stay here, something's wrong. That door is ajar," he pointed out, nodding his head toward a door that looked more like it had been torn from its hinges than was *ajar*. "I also hear an alarm going off in there."

Panic shot through Jody. Alicia was in there and something could go wrong. She itched to run into the building, but knew she wouldn't be making it more than a step out of the truck before Zeke had her back in it.

"I'm going to check it out," Zeke announced, giving her a warning look telling her exactly where she was supposed to be going. Nowhere. "Stay. Put," he ordered sternly.

"You have five minutes. If you don't come back out to get me in five minutes, I'm coming after you," Jody warned.

Zeke let out an exasperated sigh, but neither relented nor pushed the matter. He hopped out of the truck, and with the door open, the blaring alarm was much louder. Zeke stood still for a moment, cocking his head to the side, then moved forward through the door at an alarming speed. Holy shit that man could move fast. Something was very wrong. Jody glanced at the clock, taking note of the time so she could run after him in five minutes.

Bouncing her legs nervously, Jody watched the clock. Literally watched the numbers flick over. After two minutes, that was it. She could wait no longer. She knew she'd promised to wait a full five minutes, but she wasn't feeling the most patient right now. Especially knowing how quickly Zeke could move, he should have been back already.

Hopping down from the truck, Jody swiftly made her way to the door. The alarm was still on full force, and she half-wondered if she should shut it to cut off the noise. Although, by the looks of that door, it may never close again.

Inside, she stopped and listened for voices or any clues which might lead her in the direction of Zeke and her sister. It was impossible to hear anything over the clamor of the alarm, so she headed farther into the building and away from the incessant noise. When she reached a small room that reminded her distinctly of a common room from the *Harry Potter* movies, she took in the lived-in look of everything. A blanket was strewn across the couch and she wondered if that's where Alicia had been sleeping the last several nights.

Shouting from the direction of one of the hallways captured Jody's attention and she gingerly made her way toward them.

"Fucking bitch," a man's voice yelled, and Jody prayed it wasn't directed at her sister.

Jody picked her pace up to a run, and slowed just before reaching a door where the voices were much louder.

"Princess," a voice hissed, and she looked up to see Zeke crouched low on the other side of the entry.

The look he gave her was scathing, but she wasn't about to back down. Something was happening in there, and she just *knew* her sister was in danger.

In a flash, Zeke was next to her and pulling her back around the corner into a little kitchenette. His timing was impeccable, since they'd barely slipped around before a Vampire led Alicia's coworker Jackie into the lab. Jody had only met her once when the three of them had gone out for drinks, but she had no idea what the other woman was doing here. Were they trying to use her as leverage when they'd lost Jody?

"What's going on?" Jody mouthed to Zeke, hoping he could read lips.

Zeke didn't have time to answer before he pulled her tight to the wall again to avoid being seen when another set of Vampires dragged two limp bodies through the door. One of them she recognized as Jackson. Jody's panic ratcheted up a few notches. If Jackson was unconscious, or dead, what state was Alicia in?

"Breathe," Zeke whispered in her ear when her panic began stealing her oxygen.

"Don't worry, they're not dead. Yet. We still have business with them," a sinister voice Jody now most definitely recognized as Micelli's carried from the lab.

Micelli was here, it was him and his men who had broken in and were causing all the chaos.

"Shoot her," Micelli's voice rang out. Jody let out a little gasp. No, it couldn't be Alicia.

A moment later the unmistakable sound of a gunshot echoed through the building.

"No!" Jody screamed, and not even the steely arms of Zeke could keep her from her sister.

Tearing through the doorway, Jody was glad her unexpected entrance kept the Vampires in the room in a state of surprise. The sight of her sister bleeding on the floor put her training to the forefront of her mind. Falling to the floor next to Alicia, Jody immediately placed her hands over the wound, trying to stanch the flow of blood. The location of the wound meant a whole lot of things could go wrong, and with it the chances of survival plummeted.

Jody heard a shout from behind her and the sickening crunch of bone breaking and the accompanying scream, but she didn't bother looking to see who was injured now. Her focus was solely on Alicia.

"Please," she pleaded, looking up to where Micelli towered over her. "Please call an ambulance."

Micelli barked out a laugh. "So nice to see you turned up after all." He scowled down at her. "Someone lock her in a room somewhere. Him, too," Micelli said, directing Jody's attention to where a bleeding Zeke was being held by two of Micelli's Vampire guards.

Another Vampire gripped Jody around the middle and wrenched her away from Alicia. She grappled to place her hands back over the wound, but the Vampire was merciless.

"No!" she screamed as she watched blood continue to leak from the wound. It was fatal, but she *knew* if she could get one of the Vampires to give their blood Alicia would recover just fine. "Please, give her some blood. Please!" she pleaded while the Vampire dragged her across the room.

Jody's eyes were glued to her sister lying prone on the floor. Her dying sister. A sob broke loose and she continued to beg and plead for Micelli and his band of unsavory Vampires to save Alicia. Jody could barely hear his laughing over her screams.

"That's enough out of you," the Vampire holding her captive announced when she cleared the doorway where she could no longer see Alicia.

A sharp pain burst across the back of her head and the world went dark.

IRREVERSIBLE

Old enemies emerge from the shadows, storming the Vampires' lab, halting testing on the preliminary formulation of the cure for Vampirism. As the twisted web of events dating back to Endre's incarceration beneath the earth begins to unravel, the Vampires learn they have merely been pawns in an elaborate revenge scheme.

When all hell breaks loose, the life of one of their own is cut short and a deadly new creature is spawned, sparking awareness of side-effects of the cure.

In a startling turn of events, unlikely allies come to the rescue, allowing the Vampires to continue their work to create a viable serum in an attempt to reverse the effects of Vampirism.

TARA IS A WICKEDLY TALENTED WRITER WHO LIVES IN THE FROZEN NORTH IN MINNESOTA WITH HER WONDERFUL HUSBAND AND TWO RAMBUNCTIOUS LITTLE DUDES. SHE IS AN ENGINEER DURING THE DAY, A CRAZY MOM IN THE AFTERNOON AND A WRITER AT NIGHT. SHE ENJOYS SPENDING HER TIME PLAYING IN THE DIRT WHEN HER GARDENS AREN'T COVERED IN SNOW AND LISTENING TO A WIDE VARIETY OF MUSIC THAT INSPIRES HER WRITING — SOMETIMES DOING BOTH AT THE SAME TIME.

CONTACT TARA

- EMAIL -
TARAVASSER.AUTHOR@GMAIL.COM

- FACEBOOK –
WWW.FACEBOOK.COM/TARAVASSERAUTHOR

- WEBSITE –
HTTP://WWW.AUTHORTARAVASSER.COM

- TWITTER -
WWW.TWITTER.COM/TARAVASSER

- GOODREADS -
WWW.GOODREADS.COM/AUTHOR/SHOW/153
25170.TARA_VASSER

Other Books By Tara

The Bloodlust Chronicles
Irresistible – Book 1
Irredeemable – Book 2
Irreplaceable – Book 3
Irrecoverable – Book 4
Irrepressible – Book 5
Irreversible – Book 6
Irrevocable – Book 7